Amanda looked down at the man asleep on the sweet-smelling grass, and the temptation began to play with her.

Just one small kiss. He would never know.

She studied the curve of his cheek, the squareness of his jaw, noticed, again, the dark crescents of tiredness under his eyes.

It was the vulnerability she saw in him, rather than his familiar strength, that finally made her give in to the temptation.

She moved close to him. Touched the familiar silk of his hair with her fingertips. Brushed her lips over his cheek.

An awful truth hit her then. She had loved Fletcher Harris always. And she loved him still. Loving him and losing him had nearly killed her the first time—the final blow to a heart so racked with pain it could hardly go on.

Could she survive loving him again?

Dear Reader,

Have you started your spring cleaning yet? If not, we have a great motivational plan: For each chore you complete, reward yourself with one Silhouette Romance title! And with the standout selection we have this month, you'll be finished reorganizing closets, steaming carpets and cleaning behind the refrigerator in record time!

Take a much-deserved break with the exciting new ROYALLY WED: THE MISSING HEIR title, *In Pursuit of a Princess,* by Donna Clayton. The search for the missing St. Michel heir leads an undercover princess straight into the arms of a charming prince. Then escape with Diane Pershing's SOULMATES addition, *Cassie's Cowboy.* Could the dreamy hero from her daughter's bedtime stories be for real?

Lugged out and wiped down the patio furniture? Then you deserve a double treat with Cara Colter's *What Child Is This?* and Belinda Barnes's *Daddy's Double Due Date.* In Colter's tender tearjerker, a tiny stranger reunites a couple torn apart by tragedy. And in Barnes's warm romance, a bachelor who isn't the "cootchie-coo" type discovers he's about to have twins!

You're almost there! Once you've rounded up every last dust bunny, you're really going to need some fun. In Terry Essig's *Before You Get to Baby...* and Sharon De Vita's *A Family To Be,* childhood friends discover that love was always right next door. De Vita's series, SADDLE FALLS, moves back to Special Edition next month.

Even if you skip the spring cleaning this year, we hope you don't miss our books. We promise, this is one project you'll love doing.

Happy reading!

Mary-Theresa Hussey

Mary-Theresa Hussey
Senior Editor

Please address questions and book requests to:
Silhouette Reader Service
U.S.: 3010 Walden Ave., P.O. Box 1325, Buffalo, NY 14269
Canadian: P.O. Box 609, Fort Erie, Ont. L2A 5X3

What Child Is This?

CARA COLTER

SILHOUETTE *Romance*®

Published by Silhouette Books

America's Publisher of Contemporary Romance

To my beautiful niece,
Amey "Amers" Sarvis,
with love

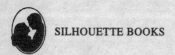 SILHOUETTE BOOKS

ISBN 0-373-19585-0

WHAT CHILD IS THIS?

This edition published by arrangement with Harlequin Books S.A.

® and TM are trademarks of Harlequin Books S.A., used under license.
Trademarks indicated with ® are registered in the United States Patent
and Trademark Office, the Canadian Trade Marks Office and in other
countries.

Visit Silhouette at www.eHarlequin.com

Printed in U.S.A.

CARA COLTER

shares ten acres in the wild Kootenay region of British Columbia with the man of her dreams, three children, two horses, a cat with no tail and a golden retriever who answers best to "bad dog." She loves reading, writing and the woods in winter (no bears). She says life's delights include an automatic garage door opener and the skylight over the bed that allows her to see the stars at night.

She also says, "I have not lived a neat and tidy life, and used to envy those who did. Now I see my struggles as having given me a deep appreciation of life, and of love, that I hope I succeed in passing on through the stories that I tell."

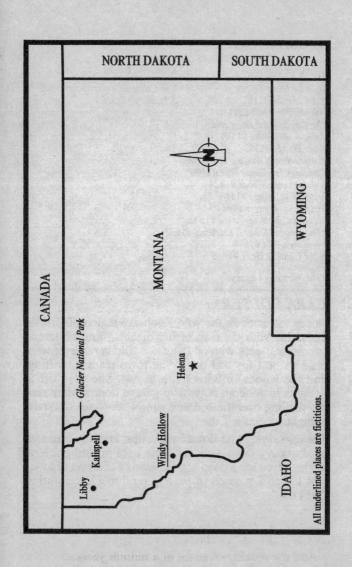

CANADA

NORTH DAKOTA

SOUTH DAKOTA

Glacier National Park

Libby

Kalispell

MONTANA

WYOMING

Windy Hollow

Helena ★

IDAHO

All underlined places are fictitious.

Chapter One

Fletcher Harris did not like spring. He particularly did not like the month of May. And for a lot of good reasons. It meant summer was coming, and there was still no air-conditioning in any of the Windy Hollow patrol cars. Upgrading the vehicles was not in the town budget this year. Or the next, as far as he could tell.

This coming weekend, his grandmother, who just turned eighty-one, would want to plant her garden. She would have flowers in the front of her house, annuals to be sown among the perennials, a new bed or two she wanted dug and flower pots to be filled and moved at least a dozen times before she was satisfied.

Around the back, in her massive yard, she would want rows strung for peas and carrots and beans and beets and seed potatoes. She would want the screens put on, and the walks sprayed down, and maybe a fresh coat of paint on her shutters.

And she would not admit in a million years she was

no longer sprightly enough to take on these projects herself.

In the spring young men became reckless and drove too fast and drank too much and tried to outdo themselves in feats of daring. In the spring young men threw themselves into that primal competition: strongest, fastest, toughest.

In the spring young women shortened their skirts and showed their belly buttons and allowed themselves to feel the pull of things dangerous. In the spring young women fell under the spell of rippling young muscles and devil-may-care smiles.

No, Fletcher Harris did not like spring. He was oblivious to ice going out of the rivers, the snow line creeping higher and higher up the Bitterroot Mountains. He did not care for blossoms and delicate shades of green. As winter lifted and the days lengthened and grew warmer, his spirit grew inexplicably darker. And that did not bode well for the bad guys.

It was May 21 today, and unreasonably hot for this northern part of Montana. Of course, he was parked in his cousin Brian's black pickup truck. The seats were black vinyl, the steering wheel was black, every single item in the vehicle was designed to attract and capture heat.

Fletcher had parked in the shade of a huge maple in the morning, but that shadow had long since moved on. It was probably over one hundred degrees in the vehicle. If he was a dog, the Humane Society would have rescued him by now. He looked longingly toward the snow that still capped the highest peaks of the Bitterroots.

He'd borrowed the pickup to do a little surveillance.

Windy Hollow did not have a surveillance car, nor was there any sense getting one.

Within a few days, everyone would know which car it was, and would be waving cheerfully at Fletch, no matter how hard he worked on not being seen.

His cousin lived in Belleview, thirty miles to the north and had been delighted to trade his '83 Ford for the '99 silver Pathfinder, Fletcher's personal vehicle, for a few days.

No, despite the heat, the black pickup was perfect. Dirty, dented, unobtrusive. It fit in totally with the other vehicles parked along the curbless lane in this working-class neighborhood where loggers and roofers and painters resided. And, in a plaid shirt and faded jeans, he fit in, too. Of course, he knew how loggers looked. His father had been one, and Fletch himself had done a fair bit of work in the timber, B.A.

Before Amanda.

He frowned. He had promised himself he would not think of her today, not even with the rumors that things between her and that doctor she was dating were heating up. The gossip was already spreading through town like the wildfires they would live in fear of if summer was hot and dry again this year.

That was the problem with surveillance. Way too much time to think.

If they were dealing dope out of 1057 Church Street, he hoped it would be revealed to him soon. He was aware the anonymous tip could well be a prank or the malicious trick of a disgruntled girlfriend.

So far, Fletcher had seen no activity around the house. Still, the warning signs were all there. The yard and house had that look of neglect: newspapers ignored on the front stoop; the main window boarded up;

weeds, waist-high instead of lawn. More attention had been paid to the fence, high and recently patched, than to the dwelling. Every now and then, through the rotting slats, he caught sight of a rottweiler prowling restlessly on the end of a thick chain.

Suspicious, but hardly enough to get a warrant.

His pager vibrated in his inside pocket. He had the sound turned down, in yet more effort not to call attention to himself through the open windows of the truck. Anyone paying attention would know a *real* logger wouldn't be sitting in his truck in the middle of the day yakking on a cell phone.

He'd told Jenny, the aging dispatcher, only to contact him in case of emergency. Still, he was aware her interpretation of an emergency differed from his. For Jenny, emergency had various meanings. Herbert Solenberg's blue ribbon rabbit had escaped again. Someone had snitched Leila Evanshaw's bra off her line. Also again.

He didn't call in.

After three minutes the pager began to vibrate once more. It was like having a fly in a jar in his pocket. He got the idea. He could call in or be tormented by more than heat. He considered hurling the pager out the window, recognized that impulse as his own spring madness, and reluctantly slid his cell phone out of his pocket.

He pulled his baseball cap down lower over his eyes, slouched in the seat, and punched the numbers for the station.

"Windy Hollow Police."

The cheer in Jenny's voice made it damned apparent that the liquor store had not been held up, and no one was threatening to jump from the top floor of the Wilton Hotel, the tallest building in town at three stories.

"Fletch," he said tersely. In his rearview mirror he saw a car pull into the 1057 driveway. The dog howled menacingly. He sank a little lower in the seat.

"Hello, Fletcher." Her sweet voice held just a touch of reprimand. Getting straight to business was not Jenny's strong suit.

How could he get mad at her? It would be like getting mad at his grandmother—who would also consider it exceedingly bad manners to use a name instead of a more conventional greeting.

In his side view mirror, he watched as two young men got out of the car, looked around carelessly, and went up the steps. Still, they had looked around. The door of the house opened a crack, then wider. The two slid in.

"Fletcher?"

"Hello, Jenny," he answered, reluctantly, glancing at his watch.

"Are you enjoying this beautiful day?"

"Not particularly."

"Now, that is a shame!" She began to tell him about her backyard flowers. He kept his eyes on the side mirror.

The young men were back out already. Another quick glance at his watch. Thirty seconds. Laughing, the driver tossed something to the passenger and they both got in the vehicle, then roared out of the driveway right past where he was parked.

He looked hard at the occupants of the car, and recognized neither of them. He jotted down the license number of the vehicle.

"Jenny, put out a call over the radio for the guys to

be on the lookout for a green Nova. Older model. Maybe an '83 or '84.'' He read out the license number. "Two guys, both blond, early twenties, one has on a red Flames cap. Pull them over on any excuse—speeding, light out, no signal. Look for drugs.''

Jenny hissed through her teeth, still indignant over any kind of wrongdoing in *her* town, even after all these years of working for the tiny police department. She'd been there thirty years, which was twenty more than Fletch, and he suspected he would retire before she did.

To his annoyance, she left the phone, and put out the call over the radio while he waited, drumming his fingers on the hot steering wheel.

She came back in a moment. "Is that all, chief?''

"You called me,'' he reminded her, managing the smallest vestige of patience. "An emergency?''

"There is a parcel for you at the bus station.''

He bit back the sigh. "I'll get it when I'm done here.''

"Thelma just called and said you need to get it now. It's perishable.''

The sweat trickled down the back of his neck. "I didn't order anything perishable. Did you?''

"No. But maybe you have a friend who sent you something.'' She mulled this over momentarily. "Live lobster! Wouldn't that be great?''

He was not sure how her mind had made the leap from perishable to live lobster, but the fact that it had helped him understand why he could never find anything in the files without her help. And it let him know that he might as well quit trying.

She should know by now he didn't have any friends, but she was an incurable and hopeless optimist. Jenny was a big fan of spring, too. In another day or two she'd have big bouquets of lilacs all over the station house. He didn't think a police station was an appropriate place for spring flowers, but his protests fell on deaf ears.

He let the sigh out and glanced again in the side mirror. A kid with uncombed blond hair and a big tattoo on his forearm was coming out of the yard. He was in a T-shirt with a marijuana leaf proudly embossed on the front of it. The rottweiler lunged and slathered at the end of a flimsy-looking leash. The kid shot a look at the truck, a little longer than Fletch would have liked. Time to leave.

Now that it had been spotted, the black pickup wouldn't work again for surveillance. Fletch considered the possibility that he might be able to come back if he shaved and wore sunglasses. Whose car could he borrow?

Glancing once more in the rearview, imprinting on his brain the face of the boy being dragged along by the dog, he started the truck, pulled out and turned the fan on high.

It blew hot air on him, but even that felt better than the stifling stillness of moments ago.

The bus station was three minutes away, but then what wasn't three minutes away in Windy Hollow?

The bus station was a squat brick building located under the spreading branches of a giant Crimson King maple that had been planted way back when the hollow had still been windy.

Fletch got out of the truck, felt the stiffness in his legs and back, and stretched mightily. Thelma Theobald was watching him hungrily from behind the window, and he stopped stretching before he wanted to.

Thelma was one of those women with a police-thing. He wondered suspiciously if she'd brought him here on a pretense.

Perishable? Like a container of Häagen-Dazs he hoped.

Given how overheated he felt, it would be a lot harder to resist than Thelma, whom he had been successfully resisting for as long as he could remember.

He pasted his best hard, cold, mean look on his face hoping it would deter her and opened the door. The air-conditioning felt wonderful, but he was careful not to let his pleasure show in his face.

"Hi, Fletch." Her voice dripped syrup, and in honor of spring, her shirt ended just short of her belly button.

He nodded. Thelma was a nice-looking woman, always had been. But he was ruined for nice-looking women. And had been for a long, long time. Maybe he was just plain old ruined.

"Got something for me?" His voice had enough ice and authority in it to discourage any kind of flirting or flaunting.

Thelma, some wicked amusement dancing in her eyes, nodded over his shoulder.

He turned slowly, and saw nothing behind him. A candy bar machine, a notice board and a little girl sitting on a bench.

He nearly turned back to Thelma, but the little girl captured his attention. She only looked to be five or six. Her head was bent, and her thin shoulders were hunched under the straps of a worn-looking pair of denim overalls. A shock of light-brown hair was pulled up into a funny little ponytail right at the top of her head.

"I didn't think you should keep her waiting any

longer,'' Thelma said softly. ''Poor tyke looks about done in.''

He whirled and gave Thelma an incredulous look. ''Waiting for what?''

It was Thelma's turn to look incredulous. ''You. It's right there on her overalls.''

He turned slowly back. The little girl was peeping at him now, but she looked swiftly back down when he looked at her. He had caught a glimpse of eyes so blue they reminded him of a swimming hole he used to go to where sunlight filtered through trees and glinted off water a shade of blue so deep and cool you could get lost in it.

It was a place he used to go a long time ago. Before he was ruined.

His eyes found the tag pinned with a large safety pin to her overalls, the paper partly bent over. Enough showing for him to see this wasn't one of Thelma's attention-getting schemes.

To: Fletcher Harris, Windy Hollow.

He had a million questions to ask Thelma. What bus had she come in on? Where from? What time? Who had been the driver? Where was her ticket?

But Fletcher could see the terror and pain in those huge blue eyes, and the tracks of dried tears on cheeks that were round and sweet, despite the gauntness of the girl's small frame. The plump bottom lip trembled helplessly. His questions for Thelma would have to wait.

He went to the child slowly, squatted down in front of her, not letting on that his stiff limbs protested from it.

''Hi, sweetheart,'' he said. His voice sounded way

too gruff to him, and the words sounded like a man stumbling with the first syllables of a foreign language.

The girl shot him a look, then looked quickly away.

He took that to mean he had missed the sincere, compassionate note he had been trying for. By a county mile.

"I'm a policeman." He tried again. "It's okay to talk to me."

She shot him another quick look, a skeptical one. She obviously had some idea what a policeman looked like, and it was not him.

Unshaven, ball cap over unruly hair, stained work shirt and jeans—all part of the look he'd thrown together this morning to avoid drawing attention to himself in the blue-collar neighborhood where he'd been watching that house.

He pulled out his wallet, and gently moved the ID card and badge into her frame of vision. "See?" he said. "I'm a policeman. You can ask Thelma over there behind the counter."

He looked sternly at Thelma. No time to play games.

Thelma got the hint and nodded vigorously. "It's true, honey. Fletcher Harris is the law in Windy Hollow."

The little girl shriveled up a little more.

"You're not in any kind of trouble," he assured her. "I just need to ask you some questions."

"You mean you weren't expecting her, Fletch?" Thelma said. "Jeez, I figured she must be a niece or something. Your brother has kids, right?"

"My sister. But this isn't one of them."

As if he had rejected her personally, a little tear sprouted in the corner of the child's eye, spilled down her cheek and fell off her chin.

"Hey, sweetheart, it's okay. There's just been some kind of mix-up. It's not your fault." When that didn't get her attention, he reached over and touched her shoulder, feeling like a grizzly bear trying to be gentle with a buttercup.

The child took a deep and shuddering breath, and then nearly knocked him over when she flung herself off the bench and against his chest. For a moment he froze, feeling her tears splash down his shirt and the scrawny strength in the arms that wrapped around his neck.

Slowly, gingerly, he put his arms around her and held her tight to him. His legs were giving out, so he straightened and stood up, taking her with him.

She weighed nothing. Her tears were soundless. Her breath, the rise and fall of her chest, reminded him of a tiny bird fallen from its nest.

He walked over to the counter. "How long has she been here?" he asked quietly over her head.

"Since I called the station. This morning." Thelma said this defensively, with an edge to it.

"Did you tell Jenny there was a child here?"

"For God's sake, Fletcher, I thought you were expecting her. I was trying to be funny when I said your special little parcel had arrived."

He bit back his impatience. A child abandoned and hours lost in trying to find answers. Still, he could feel the little girl trembling against him, and knew now was not the time to pursue it. If he showed his real colors to Thelma he'd scare the little girl nearly to death, and he needed her to trust him.

"Look, I'm going to take her across the street and get her a hamburger." He didn't add he was going to pry her life story out of her, getting her guard down with milkshakes and French fries. "You get Jenny on the phone and tell her I need to know what town this kid got on the bus, and who put her on it. I need the driver. I need the bus ticket. I need whomever she sat next to on the bus, whomever she might have talked to."

Thelma nodded. "I think I can reach the driver on the radio system."

"Good. You do that. Call me or Jenny as soon as you have anything."

The little girl had stopped crying and was listening avidly. He set her down, and she swiped at her eyes with the back of a dirty sleeve.

"What's your name?" he asked her, putting his hands on his knees and bending over so he could be the same height as her, looking her straight in those eyes.

Silence.

"Are you hungry?" he asked.

She nodded solemnly, and when he put out his hand she took it, hard, like he had thrown her a lifeline.

"No wonder I thought she was related to you," Thelma said. "Look at those eyes."

He glared at Thelma, just to let her know he knew exactly where every unfounded rumor in all of Windy Hollow originated, and then turned and walked his little charge across the street to the Windy Hollow Diner and Café. He always thought one name or the other would do, but, like lilacs in the police station, you gave up trying to change things after awhile.

He ordered them both hamburgers, and a milkshake and fries for the little girl, then watched her inhale them, while he ignored the waitress, Francine's, curious looks.

"I have a niece. She's seven. How old are you?" He was scraping through his mind for the right thing to say, the thing that would put her at ease.

The girl regarded him solemnly, hesitated, held up four fingers, and then as an afterthought included her thumb.

"You're five?" he asked.

She nodded.

"My niece's name is Sarah. What's yours?"

Nothing.

"Is the milkshake good?"

Vigorous nod.

"Do you want another one?"

Another vigorous nod.

He tried every trick in the book to get something, anything out of her. Not one peep. Of course, his book didn't include interrogation techniques for five-year-olds.

After she was done her lunch, she stared at him while he talked. Or tried to talk. Her eyelids drooped. And then without a bit of warning, her body went limp and she slid under the table and onto the floor.

He scrambled over to her and picked her up, aware again of the featherlightness of her, the fragility. He stared down at her helplessly. Had the kid fainted? Was she sick?

Then she nestled into his arms, and a soft snore escaped her. He saw the dark circles under her eyes, the exhausted pallor of her skin. She wasn't sick. She was tired. Worn right out.

What now? Mrs. Gauthier. He went out to the truck and noticed the heat as soon as he opened the passenger side door. But she didn't. She didn't even stir as he laid her carefully on the seat, and then went around to the other side and climbed in.

He knew, suddenly and without question, he could not take the little girl to Mrs. Gauthier's, who usually did their temporary care. It was too loud there. And way too crowded. Usually with kids who knew a thing or two about mean streets. Besides, Mrs. Gauthier was competent and efficient, but she always looked over-burdened. She wouldn't have an ounce of tenderness to spare for this little mite.

Flicking on the ignition, he knew where he was taking her, though it bothered his logical mind that he didn't know why.

Why would he take her there?

To that big, quiet house on the hill, no doubt surrounded by flowers at this time of year.

She would come to the door, all grace and composure. What if he caught a whiff of her scent? Lemons and sunshine.

He had not seen her, except at a distance for years. That took a lot of doing in a town this size. But he knew himself and his own weaknesses, and the aroma of Amanda might be enough to finish him completely.

She still looked wonderful, even at a distance. Tall and willowy, that red hair spilling in a wave she could never quite tame all the way down to the center of her back. She walked with that same swinging, I-own-the-earth stride that had first caught his attention, made him notice that Amanda Cooper, the doctor's daughter, was all grown-up.

God. Fourteen years ago? Fifteen? They'd both been in high school.

She'd never remarried. No, she was the epitome of the career woman now. Teaching at the community college, driving her brand-new bright red VW bug, always dressed in the muted pastel suits with skirts that were never too short, tasteful gold jewelry at her throat.

She had remodeled the old Flanders place, she had started the breakfast club for the high school, and she had spearheaded a literacy program.

And only someone who knew her as well as he once had would ever see the sadness in her huge green eyes. Even from a distance.

Of course, now the rumor was buzzing about her and the new doctor in town. Maybe that would put the laughter back in her eyes.

He burned just thinking about it.

He knew it was crazy to take this little lost child there, to Amanda Harris, the woman who had been with him when spring lost its magic.

Forever.

And he also knew he could take her nowhere else.

He was compelled, pulled by an invisible wire, to bring the little girl up the hill to the house of a woman he had not spoken to for four years. His ex-wife's house.

It was only when he'd stopped in front of it and gotten out of the truck, shutting the door gently behind him so as not to wake the sleeping child, that he felt foolish. It was painfully obvious to him that Amanda had gone on with her life. That while he hid out in a little cabin on a weedy acre down by the river, ruined, she was anything but.

He had nursed the illusion that it meant something that she had never reverted to her maiden name. But he saw now he'd only been kidding himself.

He had stayed stuck. She had moved on.

Had he come here because of that stupid rumor about her and the doctor? Hoping? For what?

He had never been this close to her house before, though the whole town had raved about its restoration—thought it should have been put on that PBS show "New Heart for Old Homes."

It was beautiful. The picture in the paper had not done it justice. Two stories high, the wooden siding sparkled white. There were green shutters around the windows. The house was embraced by a wide, cool wraparound porch, the wide floor slats painted green. Her flowers were out already in tubs and hangers, everywhere.

His grandmother said planting before May 24 was risky in this part of the country, where late frosts were common, but then Amanda had always had a little part of her that liked to live dangerously. A part that once he had been the only one who knew about.

An unvarnished cedar glider sat under the front window, plump green flowered cushions on it.

Looking at that swing he knew he was not ready to be here. Not nearly.

Because he could not look at her swing without wondering if she sat on it in the moonlight. What she thought of. If it was of him.

Or if someone else sat on the swing with her now. The doctor. It felt, absurdly, like some kind of slap in the face that she had found her way back to her own kind of people, the kind of lifestyle she had grown up with.

The house seemed huge for one person. It seemed like the kind of house someone who wanted a family would buy and lovingly restore. It seemed like a house that cried for a swing set in the massive yard and a trike on the porch.

Feeling suddenly terribly unsure of why he was here, aware of some pain burning in the region of his heart, he turned to get back in the truck. Only it was too late. He heard the screen door whisper open.

Too late as he remembered what he looked like and what he was driving. He wished for his uniform, crisp and official looking, as if somehow that would offer him protection, something to hide behind.

And he wished he had a patrol car, or his own vehicle. One might say he was here on official business, and that he wasn't quite the loser he appeared to be.

He sighed. Not thinking things quite through was his specialty around Amanda. It had been right from the beginning. At the ripe old age of nineteen, if he had thought things through, he would have never taken a seventeen-year-old bride.

He braced himself and turned slowly back.

She was standing on the porch, her hands on the wide railing, watching him. He knew if she was seventeen, and he was nineteen, he would make all the same mistakes all over again. Because she took his breath away, and made his heart stop beating in his chest, the same way she had always done.

Though she didn't look the same way she always had.

He noticed, first, that she had cut her hair. It swung at her shoulders now, still faintly untamed, though it made her into a woman, erasing totally and irrevocably the girl she had once been.

He did not want to think of that girl.

Laughter-filled, carefree, her eyes dancing with an inner light. A girl who had trusted him with her life.

A trust he had proved himself completely unworthy of.

Unworthy still, because instead of thinking of the words that needed to be said between them, he noticed her lips.

Painted a soft shade of peach.

They had tasted like that. Like peaches, ripe and juicy, the taste of summer and promises and passion.

The freckles were already darkening over the little curve of her nose. She had always been self-conscious about the bump on it, where she had broken it skiing.

Somehow he had loved the imperfection in her.

Knowing perhaps, even then, in the beginning, that she was perfect and he was not. That she would walk with the gods, and he would stay chained to mere mortals.

She had been everything *more* than him. Smarter. Classier. At ease with people. Charming.

That classiness had matured in her; she wore it now like a part of her skin. She used makeup differently. Had she used it at all, back then? Now the expert and subtle smudges around her eyes made them look larger and deeper and greener than he had remembered, and he could have sworn he remembered her eyes best of all.

She was wearing a green blouse, a shade of emerald that matched her eyes perfectly and that clung softly even while it shouted, *hands off.* Without ever having been around much silk, he knew that's what it was, and wondered what it would be like to feel it.

She had on white trousers that ended just below her knees and hugged the swell of her hips, showing off the sensual curves of her legs. Although she was still slender, she had somehow lost the bony litheness of her youth, filling out in ways and places that made his mouth go dry.

Her feet were bare, and he knew it was stupid to find that erotic, but he did, and when he looked back up into the liquid greenness of her eyes, and caught a tantalizing hint of her scent on the spring breeze, he felt that familiar charge in the air between them.

A charge that had made a rich girl leave her family for a poor boy with no prospects. A charge that had carried them through those first years when they had been so young and so poor, and so full of dreams. Crazy for each other, exhausted, he from working two jobs, her from going to college, they had lived on macaroni and hot dogs in a basement suite they shared with a mouse that she named. How could those days shimmer now in memory with a light almost holy?

"You remembered," she said softly.

It took him totally off guard. Remembered what? Could she see what was in his eyes? The ache to hold her? To taste her? To turn back the clock? To be young again with her and so crazy in love nothing else could touch them? Nothing else could matter?

His eyes caught on the gold chain on her slender neck. It glittered in the sun, and a locket swung on the end of it. He knew, with a sinking feeling, the picture that locket held.

And then he knew how undeserving he was of the tenderness in Amanda's voice.

He felt a shiver go up and down his spine. May 21. His daughter's birthday. She would have been, he despised himself for having to stop and think about it, nine.

If she had lived.

And Fletcher knew a truth he had been running from

all spring. The reason he hated this time of year was not so inexplicable after all.

It was in the spring that he had found out that everything he thought he was—strongest, fastest, toughest—had only been the most painful of illusions.

Chapter Two

Amanda Harris's first thought was *Oh, Fletch, not now*. It was too late. Sometimes, now, she could sleep through the night without dreaming of his arms, strong as steel bands, holding her. Sometimes, now, she could see a young man smile, reckless and devil-may-care, and not think of the way Fletch used to be.

She was finally putting her life back together. Woodall was such a nice man. Steady and calm. It was only this very instant, with Fletch at the bottom of her stairs, that she realized Woodall was the man least likely to trigger memories. He was Fletch's polar opposite in every way. Looks, attitude, lifestyle.

She studied Fletch's image, and decided he looked terrible. His face was rough with dark whiskers, his jet-black hair ragged with sweat where it protruded out from under a paint-splattered ball cap, his jeans in tatters, the shirt too small for his big frame.

For all that, right underneath the whiskers and the rags was Fletch, so ruggedly attractive, so purely and uncompromisingly masculine that there was not another man alive who made Amanda feel this way. Her heart beating in her throat, her palms suddenly slick, a dark, hot *wanting* uncurled in her stomach, like a tigress awaking from sleep, stretching, looking with urgent, hungry sensuality at him.

The whisker-shadowed cheeks could not hide the chiseled perfection of his features, the sharp angle of his cheekbones, the sweeping line of his nose, the jut of his chin. It was not so much that he was handsome, so much as he was purely *man.* Everything about him, *everything,* proclaimed raw, physical power. It was stamped in the features of his face, and then the theme repeated in the column of his neck, in the broad swell of big shoulders, the solid expanse of chest, the thick squareness of his wrists, the hard line of a flat stomach, the firm plant of long, powerful legs.

Seeing him, memory reminded her she *knew* the taste of his skin, and the way his hard, sinewy muscles felt under her fingertips. It filled her with a desire to capture something lost, to travel again to those days of exhilaration that were first love.

She yanked herself away from the pure danger of these thoughts. Second love would be better. Calmer, more soothing, predictable. She liked everything about Dr. Woodall Lamb, and Fletch Harris was not going to spoil it for her simply by showing up at her doorstep.

Besides, she had been mistaken about why he was here. She could tell from the startled look on his face that he had not come because he remembered, and she could tell the precise moment he did remember it would have been Tess's birthday today.

The deep clear blue of his eyes suddenly clouded, and *that* look came into his eyes. That distant haunted look that made his features cool and remote, that drew him so far into himself he could not find his way out and she could not follow him.

Once, when she was very young, she had believed the power of their love could survive all things. She had believed it enough to defy the dire warnings of her parents about marrying beneath herself, and to scoff at the friends who had tried to tell her she was giving up something to be with him. Her youth. Her dreams. Her chances.

They thought she was giving up something. She pitied them because they just didn't *know* about hard hands on soft skin, and hot kisses on cold nights. They didn't know that some things were worth giving up, depending on what you received in exchange.

But in the exuberance Fletch had brought to her life, Amanda hadn't even believed she was exchanging anything. There were no trade-offs. She believed, simply, she could have it all. Fletch. Passion. Love. Career. Family.

Now, she wondered sometimes if the very power of her belief had been like a taunt to the gods.

But when she had seen him standing outside in the spring sunshine, regarding her house with narrowed eyes, hadn't she believed again?

Just for a flash, had not some hope that she thought was long dead within her leaped rebelliously to life?

But he had not come to tell her he, too, remembered this day. He had not come to reminisce about that day they had brought a baby into the world, to feel the sadness that would bring them both or to find the healing they so desperately needed.

If he had that kind of sensitivity in him maybe they could have held it together. But he had left her. First emotionally, and then physically. That is what she needed to remember when she felt the pull of eyes bluer than Miller's Pond on the hottest summer day.

"Why are you here, Fletch?" she asked in a businesslike tone. One that she hoped disguised the aching for him she realized with self-contempt had never quite left her.

She prayed he wouldn't notice the pulse she could feel, rabbit-quick, beating in the hollow of her throat.

He looked at his feet, moved the dirt around a bit with his right foot, glanced back at her and then ran a hand through the spiky blackness of his hair and looked off into the distance. His eyelashes were as thick and sooty as chimney brushes.

It reminded her so much of the very first time.

"Amanda Cooper, would you ever consider going out with me?" He had a reputation as a wild boy, but that day he'd been endearingly shy. She had noticed his eyelashes back then, too.

And something in the glint of his eye, the quirk of his lips had captured her heart, taken it prisoner, and never, ever released it.

The whole world could change, turn, evolve in a single second. When a girl looked at a boy and saw her own destiny looking back at her when she said *yes* instead of *no*.

"Why are you here, Fletch?" she repeated.

"Uh, I guess I just made a mistake." His voice was deep, sensual as rain on naked skin. There seemed to be none of that reckless boy left in him. Still, only someone who knew him as well as she did would hear the pain in it.

But she knew he made mistakes rarely. He had come

here with a purpose. Still, he turned away from her, his hand on the door handle of that god-awful truck.

The tiniest sound came from inside his truck, like the peep of a baby bird falling from its nest. The effect of that small sound on Fletcher was galvanizing.

He threw open the door, and bent inside that truck, and when he straightened and turned back to her, she saw he had a sleepy child in his arms.

She was a tiny, little girl, scrawny, dressed in overalls nearly worn through on the seat and a shirt that was dirty. Her fine light-brown hair was scooped up in an elastic at the top of her head. When she turned and peeked at Amanda, there was no missing the tear streaks on round cheeks. Then, some fragile trust in the gesture, she lay her head on Fletcher's shoulder and stuck her thumb in her mouth, slurped on it with desperate intensity.

"She needs a place to stay for a little while," Fletcher said awkwardly.

For a full minute it didn't occur to Amanda he meant here. That he had brought the little girl to her thinking she could stay here.

When she realized his intent she felt a raw and killing fury. How dare he do this? March into her life after a four-year absence where not one word had passed between them? Not one word. She had seen him crossing the road so he didn't have to bump into her and turning his police cruiser around in the middle of the block so he didn't even have to drive by her.

And suddenly, here he was on her daughter's birthday, no, *their* daughter's birthday, with a child. Asking for a favor.

And just as she was truly getting beyond the pain, putting her life back in order, actually seeing someone.

She wanted to turn on her heel, cross her porch, slam the door and lock it. Trust Fletcher Harris to take insensitivity to new heights.

But she realized the little girl had tilted her head and was contemplating her from under her thick, spiky lashes. Her eyes were the most mesmerizing shade of blue, storm sky and dark ocean, a half shade different than what she saw in the eyes of the man who was regarding her steadily from the bottom of her steps.

Amanda looked back to the small girl, and there was no missing the confusion and pain in those enormous eyes. The child looked lost and alone.

Almost breakable she was so delicate.

Amanda's fury dissolved, though she still wondered how Fletch could put her in this position. To say that she could not take the child, right in front of the child, felt like it would be unbearably cruel. She could not be the one to add yet more weight to a burden already too heavy to be carried on the child's narrow shoulders.

And saying no, turning the child away would mean Amanda Harris was not even close to being the person she thought she was or wanted to be.

Did he know that? Had he known all that when he brought the girl here?

She forced herself to detach from his being here, from his part in this, to try to think clearly.

"Fletch who is she?"

"We don't know that yet. She came in on the bus this morning with my name pinned to her overalls. That's all we've got."

Amanda felt herself react emotionally to the child's abandonment, but struggled to remain rational. "But why bring her here? Don't you have places? Foster homes?"

"Yeah." His voice was flat but his arms tightened around the child protectively, and Amanda knew exactly what he wasn't saying: that the foster homes were grim places where such a fragile mite could be crushed.

Amanda knew it was absolutely crazy, but she knew what she was going to do.

And suddenly it seemed the spring sun brightened around the little girl, glinting gold off the hair on Fletcher's arms.

Amanda asked herself if she was going to wash every event of her life through the bitterness of her own loss? Or was she going to allow her loss to make her stronger, kinder, *more* than she had been before?

What better way to honor her daughter, Tess, than to offer the love she had learned from her to another little girl? A stranger. On the day that would have been Tess's birthday.

She could feel the ache of tears behind her eyes. Trust Fletch to somehow bring her the gift she most needed and least wanted.

"Come in," she snapped at him, softening the snap by smiling at the little girl.

The girl took her thumb out of her mouth and tentatively smiled back. Her teeth were endearingly crooked.

Amanda glanced at Fletch and saw the reluctance in his eyes. It was clear he didn't want to come in. What he wanted to do was hand her the child, tip the brim of his ball cap, and leave. She shook her head in agitation. She was not going to allow him to dump a child on her doorstep and run.

She crossed the porch and opened the screen door, not looking back, making it seem he had no choice. After a moment, she heard him coming behind her, the firm tread of his feet, up the steps and across the porch, and she gave a silent sigh of relief that he had capitulated on this small point.

But the problem with unexpected reunions, she realized, was that the tiniest of things could trigger treacherous memories: how often had she listened eagerly for the sound of his footsteps coming home from a late shift?

She held the door open for him and he hesitated, then crossed the threshold in front of her into her house.

As he passed her she caught the scent of him. He smelled of laundry soap and aftershave, and faintly, enticingly of sweat. A man smell, deep and mysterious and lingering. Another treacherous trigger.

She watched him pause and look around. Amanda recognized she yearned for him to say he liked it. She wanted him to notice the golden glowing hardwood floors and the handmade throw rugs, the cozy yellow sofas that faced each other, the way the sunbeam coming in the front window shone on the fresh flowers on the coffee table.

It wasn't until she looked at him that she knew all that time she had been working on the house, and telling her it was for herself, it hadn't been.

It had all been for him.

A place he would want to come home to.

But of course, he was never coming home to her, and she had accepted that a long time ago.

She moved past him and walked through to the kitchen. He came behind her, but she heard his footsteps falter, and she glanced back at him to see what he was looking at.

On the oak mantel above her river rock fireplace was a single picture. Tess, at two, robust and teeming over with life and energy. In the photograph she was crouched over a pile of autumn leaves, looking up at the camera, smiling. Hair dark as midnight scattered wildly around her face. Her cheeks were pink with health and her green eyes sparkled with pure mischief.

She was wearing a red jacket with a white fur-trimmed hood. The strings that tightened the hood ended with white pom-poms.

She remembered, suddenly that Fletcher had bought that jacket. He had brought it home in a box, looking sheepish, because they had still been so strapped for cash paying back student loans and saving to buy a house.

Tess had laughed and clapped her hands together and insisted on having the jacket put on immediately. She had hugged her new red self and turned in ecstatic circles. She had worn the jacket everywhere for days, even to bed.

And Amanda would look at her young husband, and know the world saw him as a man who was tough and uncompromising, and that she alone could marvel at the love that softened his features and shone in his eyes when he watched his daughter. And her, his wife.

How she remembered that feeling; those moments when she became briefly aware of her life brimming over with blessings. How she wished, now, she would have paused then, breathed it in deeply, and stayed in that moment for as long as she could. How she wished she had not rushed off to do the laundry, or to study, or to get groceries. Because now she knew it was often the things you thought were forever that were the things that were most fleeting.

"How can you look at that every day?" he asked, his voice hoarse, tearing his eyes away from the picture. He looked at her with something she did not quite understand, a look that seemed to be an unlikely combination of admiration and accusation.

"How can you not?" she asked him back, quietly.

He looked at her steadily, mulling it over. She wondered if he had any pictures of Tess, if he ever looked back at those days.

And there it was, right between them, the stalemate. Grief going different ways, pulling them in different directions—hers moving her outward, his moving him inward—until there was a gulf between them so wide that neither knew how to cross it.

No wonder he had left, their love turned to loneliness, a complete travesty of what had once been.

She pushed through the swinging café-style doors into her kitchen.

"Coffee?" she said. "Tea? Lemonade?" Anything but the pain that was so fresh between them that should have dulled with time, but had not, somehow.

Both of them, the tiny waif and the big man who held her in his arms, nodded vigorously at the offer of lemonade. The girl was looking around with exactly the look in her eyes that Amanda had hoped to see in Fletch's. A kind of reverence, an unvarnished wanting.

She had designed the kitchen to be the most cozy of spaces. A replica of the country kitchens of long ago, it contained old oak mismatched furniture, lace at the windows, a black wood-burning stove in the corner, brick floors and an assortment of old teacups on display in the antique glass-fronted cabinet.

It was only with him here that she recognized how empty the illusion was that she had created. Because those old kitchens had been about families—large gatherings and laughter, the smell of turkey cooking, children playing under the table, men sticking their fingers in the icing on the cake and licking it off.

Here, the only sign of a child was a wooden rocking horse in the corner.

And of course, that was what his eyes found, and rested on, before they drifted away, pained.

He had made that horse. Tess's first Christmas, when they couldn't afford toys from the store. She remembered him putting on the finishing touches, taking apart an old mop, his tongue stuck between his teeth, glue all over his fingers as he painstakingly attached the mane and tail. She remembered the laughter in his eyes when he'd looked up at her.

Who would look at his eyes now, so somber, so hooded, and guess what had been there once?

She poured lemonade, and then sat at the table, tucking one leg under the other and a strand of hair behind her ear. She tried to remember the look of tenderness in Woodall's eyes last night when he had dropped her off.

She tried to tell herself that was where her future now lay. But she couldn't imagine Woodall dipping his finger in a freshly iced cake and licking it off.

Fletch put the child gingerly in the chair across from Amanda, but he didn't sit down. He picked up his lemonade and prowled restlessly over to the window that looked into her backyard, and stared out at it.

How did she know he was oblivious to the flowers and all those delicate shades of green that spring brought?

Amanda steeled herself against the awareness of him that threatened to swamp her and smiled at the little girl.

"I'm Amanda Harris," she said. "Who are you?"

The little girl looked between her and Fletch's broad back. Did she know his last name? Was she connecting the two of them in her mind? If she was, she was a very smart little girl.

But she did not speak, only met Amanda's eyes with a kind of drowning helplessness that melted Amanda's heart completely. Then she noticed the tag pinned to the child's overalls.

Amanda turned her eyes to Fletch, but he wouldn't look at her.

"Is she yours?" she asked his back, doing desperate arithmetic. For two years, after Tess had died, they had tried to hold it together. Sometimes, during that time, he would disappear for days at a time. She had never thought, though, that he had betrayed her in this final way.

She saw him flinch, and then he turned. He frowned, apparently having not the slightest idea how intimidating that frown made him, how completely it erased the man-child he had been when he first came to her.

A boy of such energy and devilment and sensuality.

She studied him as he studied the girl. The truth was bald in his face. He didn't think the child was his. But he wasn't one hundred percent sure.

They had tried to hold their marriage together after Tess had gone, but the chasms kept opening deeper between them until she felt as if she could only see him at a great distance.

He had become quiet, withdrawn, and yet just below that silence, he seethed with some unspoken energy. She herself had pursued her career as if hounds howled at her heels.

And one day, the grief began to pour out of him. He

had gone crazy. Drinking and partying. Living a wild life. Pushing her further and further away.

Once she had thought their love could survive anything. And it could have. Anything except that one thing. A loss too big, a hurt too high. It had not been Amanda who had walked away, though. It had been him.

"She's a mystery," Fletch said, quietly. "She arrived in the bus station this morning, with my name pinned to her overalls. That's all I know, for now. Except that she doesn't talk. Or won't talk to me."

"And why did you bring her here?" Amanda had asked him that before, she waited to see if he would answer this time. He did but his answer revealed nothing about his motives, his *feelings*.

He finished his lemonade in one swallow, set the glass down carefully, as though he were afraid he would break it. "I don't know. You don't have to take her, if you don't want."

She felt the little girl's eyes on her face, wide and frightened, silently pleading.

"Of course she can stay here until you find her family." She reached across the table and covered that tiny hand with hers.

"Thanks, Mandy."

Nobody ever called her that. Not in her whole life. Not her mother and father, not her best friends. Certainly not Woodall. Only Fletch.

And how she had loved it once, coming from his lips.

And how surprised she was to discover she loved it still.

What was she doing? Good Lord, opening her heart

to him again? What did she think she was made of, steel and solder, instead of flesh and bones?

No, Woodall Lamb was the road to take. A smooth, quiet road. Serene. No bumps, no bruises, no torturous hills to climb. Not this time.

"I'm going to go," Fletch said. "I'll find out what I can. I'll call you."

"No." As if she would give her life over into his hands, again.

"Don't call?"

"No. You can't just turn her over and forget about her."

He was glaring at her now, that look that could turn the dark blue of his eyes to a shade that approached black. "I'm not following."

"You'll have to accept part of the responsibility. Classes are done for the spring, but I'm still marking papers. I have a personal life."

Did he really grimace when she said that?

He was frowning again, but she plunged ahead. "She'll need a few clothes. You can take her shopping."

His mouth worked, but no sound came out.

"And I have plans for the weekend." She and Woodall were going antiquing this weekend, had an auction to attend and a list of estate and garage sales over a fifty-mile radius that they planned to cover.

It had sounded so wonderful when they'd arranged it. Why was she seeing it through Fletcher Harris's eyes now?

She knew what he would have to say about such an undertaking. *Boring.*

"I promised my grandmother I'd give her a hand in her yard."

She felt another sting of loss. How she loved his grandmother. Knew it was bossy, beautiful old Teresa, the woman they had named the baby after, who had kept him from sinking completely. Kept him busy and out of trouble, made sure he had a responsibility that he couldn't run from.

"Perfect," she said tartly. "I'm sure our little friend would love to meet your grandmother. And to get a little dirty at the same time. Wouldn't you, love?"

The little girl nodded uncertainly.

One of her most predominant character defects, Amanda knew, was that she never knew when to stop.

"And when's the last time you made chocolate chip cookies, Fletcher Harris? Oh, it's true," she told the little girl, "under that tough cop exterior is a man who makes the meanest chocolate chip cookies I've ever tasted."

He was actually blushing, and Amanda recalled, poignantly, that she was the only one who knew his secrets.

"And we're going to need quite a few of those, aren't we?" Amanda asked the child.

Vigorous nod.

"So, Fletch, you better stop by the store and get the ingredients for chocolate chip cookies, because I don't stock them. And you might as well pick up something for dinner, too. Let's see. Chicken. A small fryer."

"It may not look like it," he said, "but I'm working right now." He was going to try to wriggle out of it.

"We'll see you after work, then."

And part of her, the part of her that wanted to survive, prayed that he would think of a way to wriggle out of it. Had she invited him for dinner, for God's sake?

But after looking from her to the child and back again several times, he gave his head the shake of a boxer rising up from under a hard right, and walked out the back door.

"What have I done?" she whispered, watching out her kitchen window as he went, especially in light of the fact he might have betrayed her in ways she had never contemplated before.

The little girl came soundlessly. Amanda did not know she was there until she felt the small hand slide into hers.

She crouched down. "Can't you talk, honey?"

The girl shook her head, sadly, side to side.

"Well, that's okay. I bet I can do enough talking for both of us. But what am I going to call you?"

The child looked at her trustingly.

She sighed. "I know. I'll start at *A*, and say every name I know. And if you hear yours, tug on my sleeve, okay? I even have a name book somewhere. When I run out, I'll read you some of those."

Vigorous nod.

She led the little girl out onto the back porch, and filled a small watering can for her and a large one for herself.

She showed her how to water the plants, straight through, until the water flowed out the bottom.

And then she began.

"Let's see. Angela? Abby? Adeline? Amy? Alice?"

With the little girl chortling happily beside her, she named every *A* name she could think of. And then, she moved onto *B*.

Amanda taught courses and sat on boards, made sure hungry kids got fed and illiterate ones learned to read.

She had taken this house, when it was about ready to be condemned, and nursed it back to life.

Accomplishments.

Ones she had been very proud of, too.

Now, after four years, she'd accepted several dates with Woodall. He was a nice man. They had common ground. They came from similar backgrounds.

Maybe it was never too late to make her parents happy. How they would have loved for her to become a doctor's wife.

Which, of course, was moving things along way too fast. She realized she needed to think about neither Woodall nor Fletcher right now.

She just needed to focus on watering plants, and the little girl beside her. While she named every name she could think of, Amanda felt a tender little blossom unfold inside her.

Contentment.

No, more.

Happiness.

And she hoped like hell she had the good sense and survival skills to not let one bit of her happiness be about Fletcher Harris reappearing without warning in her life.

At five there was a knock on her door and her heart pounded. But when she went to the front, it wasn't Fletcher, but Jenny, the plump and aging dispatcher from the police station.

She held out a bag of groceries. "He couldn't come. He's interrogating some young hooligans about drugs. Drugs. In Windy Hollow. It frosts me something fierce."

The little girl came and peered out from behind Amanda's leg.

"Oh, there she is. Our little mystery girl. I'm not to breathe a word about her. Fletch doesn't want her on the front page of the paper." She looked closer, drew in her breath sharply.

"He asked me to get a wee snip of her hair."

"Whatever for?"

It was the older woman's hesitation that gave her the answer. Fletch was going to check the child's DNA. Against his own, no doubt.

"Tell him he'll have to come get it himself," Amanda said, too sharply, then wished she could take it back. Why leave herself open to him at all?

"My pleasure," Jenny said. "He's not gotten over it, you know. To those of us who knew him before and knew him after, it seems as if he became someone else when your baby died."

Just what I needed to hear, Amanda thought weakly.

"He never meant to hurt you. He adored you."

"Thank you." She had hoped, for a long time, maybe someday he would even say that himself. She'd heard it from everybody else in town. But of course, he never had. Now it was too late.

"Do you think there's any chance…" Jenny's voice died away.

Amanda knew Jenny didn't finish the sentence because of the look on her face—the No Trespassing sign.

"I'm sorry," Jenny said, not in the least contrite. "None of my business, of course."

"Thanks for bringing the groceries by."

"All right. You just call if you need anything else."

But what she needed Jenny couldn't give her. No one in this town could. Though they all seemed to know with as much certainty as her just what that something was.

She sighed and shut the door. She peeked in the grocery bag—one fryer, and six packages of chocolate chip cookies.

She knew she shouldn't let him off the hook that easily. But she couldn't help it. There was just a hint of the old Fletcher in the gesture. Reluctantly, she smiled.

Chapter Three

Fletcher finished the last of the paperwork, then saved the file and turned off the computer. He glanced at the clock in his office. Nearly ten-thirty. He rolled his shoulders and tried to squeeze a knot out of the back of his neck.

The two young guys in the Nova had been carrying crack cocaine and had been only too happy to sing. The warrant had been easy after that.

There was always doubt, though. Had he moved to soon? If he had been more patient could he have nailed the supplier, too?

Was his mind clouded because the other matter seemed far more urgent to him?

So far, he'd found out the little girl had been put on the bus at Stevenson, a small town about fifty miles south of here. The name on her ticket was Carol Anne Picket, and the guardian had signed Jane Anne Picket. He suspected both names were false. Nobody dumped a kid on a virtual stranger and put their real name on the bus ticket.

Virtual because Picket didn't ring any of his memory bells, either, but he knew whoever had put the kid on the bus must know him somehow or some way.

You didn't randomly send children to people.

Was the child his? That whole period of his life, six years ago when that child would have been conceived was a fog, thick with pain. The man in him said the child was absolutely not his, that he was not capable of betraying Amanda in that way. But the cop in him ferreted out nights he could not account for, lost in a haze of whiskey and anguish.

The truth was, from the day his daughter died, Fletcher Harris had become a man who did not know who he was. He came from a long line of men who believed in their own strength. Men who had logged and ranched and who had cut this corner of Montana from a raw wilderness. He had always believed himself to belong solidly to their ranks.

Then Tess. And the discovery he was not strong.

That his dainty little wife could beat him hands down in the inner strength department. Underneath all his brawn, all his authority, he had discovered there was a fragile place in him. A place that had shattered like glass.

So, could he have betrayed Amanda?

Part of him, the old Fletch, shouted no.

The new part, cynical, skeptical of himself, said maybe. He shook off these thoughts, these self-doubts, like a bull shaking off a determined rider, forced his mind, though weary, to bend to his will and to review the file he had started.

He had spoken to the woman who had sold the ticket

in Stevenson over the phone. She gave him a pretty good description of the woman who had put the girl on the bus. She remembered her because she had been crying so hard.

At least maybe that meant she cared about the kid.

Blond, long hair, fine. Tiny build, blue eyes, dark, dark circles under them. Jeans and a T-shirt. Not from around there, the bus ticket lady had told him firmly. Might have been pretty once, but not now. Late twenties. There would only be a few million people that matched a description like that, but the police in Stevenson were going to keep an eye out for her and have a police artist work on a composite that could be circulated statewide.

He'd had Jenny checking directories as soon as they had a name, on the off chance it was real. Picket was a more common name than you might think. No Jane Anne or Carol Anne listed in this state or the adjoining ones. Big surprise. That meant someone was going to have to call all the Pickets in and around Stevenson and in an ever growing circle outward to see if they could find a clue.

No child matching the description of the small waif who had mysteriously appeared in Fletch's life had been listed recently as a missing person. Or not recently, either. He'd checked back as far as six years ago, calling up picture after depressing picture of the nation's missing babies, studying the computer age enhancements until his vision was blurred and his head was pounding and that knot in his neck was tightening up like a noose.

The phone rang. Jenny reported she had delivered the parcel to Amanda. ''But she said you could get the hair sample yourself.'' The pause seemed calculated. "She's more beautiful than ever, isn't she?''

He didn't say anything. To open up his private life to Jenny, to even hint that her input might be welcome, or that in a weak moment he could be tempted to exchange confidences with her, would make working with her even more challenging than it was now.

Which was plenty challenging. On the other hand, how many other dispatchers would deliver a few groceries for him on their own time? Would genuinely care about him the way Jenny did?

"Thanks for dropping off the groceries, Jenny.''

That moment of civility left him wide-open to be scolded about the kind of hours he was keeping. He tolerated it for as long as he could before hanging up without saying goodbye.

As if he needed Jenny to tell him he worked too long. Why not work? That's all he had left. If he worked hard enough and long enough, then he could just go home, move a heap of laundry off his unmade bed and crawl into it.

Too tired to think, to feel, to mourn, to wish.

He knew he was a man going through the motions of living, without fully engaging in life. And that had not seemed like such a bad thing, until he had made the brutally bad mistake of taking that little girl to Amanda.

Walking in that house, seeing the picture of Tess on her mantel, and the homemade rocking horse standing empty in that corner had reminded him of the sweetness of being fully engaged in life.

Why had Amanda kept the stupid rocking horse? He'd been so proud of it at the time—coming home from a long day at work to cut and sand and paste and paint. Cop to Daddy, the most pleasant of transitions.

When he'd seen that horse today, it had struck him that it looked more like a cow.

He glanced at his watch, again. Was it too late to go by Amanda's place? She was right, he couldn't just dump the kid there and not take any responsibility.

Why had he gone there, instead of to the Gauthiers'? He'd dropped off dozens of kids at the Gauthiers'. Okay, it wasn't the Waltons', but it wasn't a *bad* place. Of course, not one of those other kids had ever had his name pinned to their overalls. But plenty of them had clung to him and cried. Plenty of them had felt as if they could break his heart without half trying. He'd been a survivor enough not to let them.

What had blocked his survival instincts this time? Why had he taken this little girl's dilemma so personally?

With a little chill of shock he wondered if it was specifically because some renegade part of him wanted to tangle his and Amanda's lives together again. And why was that all of a sudden?

Because every snoop in town was keeping him posted on Amanda's progress with the doctor? Had he just grown so weary of fighting the pull of her that on the first plausible excuse he had headed up her long driveway?

Or was it because he knew he could trust her with that child, as he could trust no one else?

It wasn't what he'd told her after Tess's death, he remembered painfully. *If you'd stayed home.* The accusation finally coming out of him, a volcano erupting, the lava of his rage and pain and helplessness destroying everything in its path.

He had been the big, strong guy. The traditional male who was going to take care of everything, including his wife. And she had let him. Then out of the blue, she was going to college. Had he glimpsed, even then, she was a lot stronger than he thought? Had he been threatened by it?

The problem with inviting himself back into her life was this precisely. He was going to have to look at the very thing he least wanted to look at. Himself.

He was lucky she'd opened the door to him today, come out on her porch to see what he wanted. He had no illusions about deserving it, and of course, he had let her down.

Sighing, he got up from his desk and put on his jacket. He ordered himself to go home, but knew he wouldn't. He'd just drive to the bottom of her hill and see if Amanda's lights were on. Maybe the little girl was talking by now and had told Amanda something. It might be a good time to get that hair sample. Snip it off the little girl while she slept, not have to look at the question in those huge eyes.

Before he even turned in Amanda's drive, from the bottom of the hill, he could see the house was lit up.

A pleasant sight, the big house spilling golden light over the trees all around it. It looked like the kind of place people went home to in movies but not in real life.

At least not in his real life.

He had the little cabin down by the river that his grandparents had homesteaded in. He had slapped on a bathroom, fixed it up only enough to make it livable. His housekeeping was pathetic, his interest in the aesthetics of the place nil.

But the sound of the river moving just outside his

front door brought him a measure of peace. There was something about the water running, strong, gurgling over rocks, never ending, that soothed a question in him he had not yet asked.

Fletch picked his cell phone out of his pocket and punched in Amanda's number. He had looked it up long ago, recalled it in his mind a hundred thousand times.

It occurred to him this was the first time his fingers had actually made contact with the numbers.

"Hello?" Her voice reached into the night, as surely as the lights from her house. Strong. Sure. Calm.

He closed his eyes, the yearning was like a fire beckoning a man near frozen in out of the blizzard. He'd finally dialed the number, only to find he wanted to hang up.

Grow up, he ordered himself.

"Hello?" she said, again.

"Fletch," he said, knowing Jenny would not approve.

"Thanks for the cookies," she said, and he heard a reluctant smile in her voice. "Where are you?"

Lie. He could tell her he was at home, or at the office. But he didn't. "I'm at the bottom of your hill, looking at your lights."

"Are you coming up?"

Tell her no. "Yes. If it's not inconvenient."

"Fletch, if you were going to give a thought to inconveniencing me, I don't think that little girl would be fast asleep in the spare bed. See you in a minute." She hung up, and a second later, he saw her porch light flick on.

Slowly he put the truck into gear, giving himself instructions all the way up the hill. Keep it professional. Find out if the kid is talking. Get a sample of her hair. Leave.

What if the doctor was there? At the top, to his relief, he saw only her jaunty little red VW parked in front of her gate.

Even so, when he stood on her porch and the door opened, he didn't feel professional at all.

"Come in." She was wearing the same clothes as before, only now she had a white sweater over the green shirt. It looked soft and touchable, making him want to wrap his hands in the hem of it and tug her toward him.

The doctor probably had more finesse. Which she deserved. She was a doctor's daughter. She knew all about refined living and refined people. She could easily have been on the front cover of a magazine, she looked so comfortably and casually elegant.

He still had not changed his clothes. The shirt was binding, and he thought the forced stay in his cousin's truck-sauna hadn't made him smell too sweet, which should kill any temptation he felt to bring Amanda closer to him.

He hadn't shaved, either, although he had, reluctantly, run a comb through his hair and gotten rid of the ball cap.

Her house smelled good, like people actually lived here. He could smell garlic and chicken and the yeasty, warm scent of fresh bread.

"When's the last time you ate?" she asked, looking at him closely.

Shared history. She knew he got wrapped up in what he was doing and became so intensely focused he forgot things. Like eating and shaving.

He shrugged. He would not take her concern for him personally. She had always had a soft spot for strays.

She shook her head, held out her hand for his jacket. That small gesture reminded him, thankfully, he was a visitor here.

After dealing with his jacket she led him through to the kitchen. He kept his face deliberately expressionless even though the room tugged at some place in his heart, and it was more than the little ghostly rocking horse-cow in the corner. Music, classical guitar, played in the background. It was a room that spoke of softness and serenity.

Of normal lives.

Where people didn't eat from cans and bags. Where they actually spent time in their homes, relaxing, listening to music, reading books and cooking meals, putting a little paint here or there, hanging a picture.

Where they didn't clean guns on the kitchen table or get phone calls in the middle of the night about break-ins or spousal disagreements or armed robberies or homicides or suicides or missing teenagers.

He sat down at the kitchen table, and without asking, she brought him a plate of food. Churlishly, he would have liked to refuse it, but the aroma wafting up to his nostrils stole his resolve. He was starving. He realized the hamburger with the kid, hours and hours ago, was all he'd eaten today.

In between bites, where he tried hard not to look at her, and he noticed she tried hard not to look at him, he said, "Is she talking?"

"No."

"Her name might be Carol. Or Carol Anne." The food was good. Really good. But he didn't think it would win him any brownie points if he asked her when she had learned to cook.

God knows, she hadn't been able to back then. She'd burned everything. Impatient, the energy in her bubbling too briskly to be tamed by something so mundane as a recipe.

She didn't seem so impatient anymore, so unwilling to wait. But the impatience, the intensity that had been so disastrous in the kitchen, had translated to something else entirely in their bed.

Don't go there, he warned himself. Still, he sneaked a look at her. He noticed again that the girlish slenderness was gone. He liked what had replaced it even better. She was not heavy, not even remotely, but she had a certain roundness, a fullness—a ripeness—she had not had before. She was a girl gone to woman.

Her lipstick looked fresh. Did that mean anything? Had she freshened it for his arrival? He suddenly felt hot. And unbearably lonely.

"I don't think her name is Carol," Amanda told him. "We've already done *C*." She explained to him how she was working her way through the alphabet, even using a baby name book to try to get a response from her little charge.

"No, I didn't really think so, either. But that's what was on the bus ticket. Try Carol Anne on her tomorrow. See if you get a reaction."

"Aye, aye, sir." There was the gentlest edge of sarcasm in her voice.

"Sorry," he muttered. He willed himself to leave it there, but he didn't. "I don't deal with the finer things in life anymore, Amanda. I just snap orders and people listen to them." *Or pay the price.*

The *anymore* hung in the air between them.

Suddenly he knew what was going to happen if he sat here any longer. They would have to talk about something. And they only had one thing in common. The past.

He could not sit with Amanda and listen to sentences that began *Remember when…?*

He pushed back the plate before she had a chance to ask him if he wanted more, which he did. He got up from the table. "Could I see her? I should get that hair sample."

Strictly business.

But it wasn't. As she led him through her house, it was like being led into her soul. Every picture, every color said something about her. Her warmth was everywhere. In the lovingly polished wood, the knick-knacks, the carefully chosen antiques, the paint and wallpaper.

Everything was so *clean,* so orderly.

Luckily, she was never going to see his place. It was a disaster. Dishes in the sink. Laundry on the floor. He had his lawn mower engine apart on the kitchen counter, which was a joke since he had no intention of mowing the gently rolling bank down to the river, ever. He supposed the engine kept his mind occupied when everything else had run out.

Part of him wanted to ask how she had done this. Managed to go on, live, care about things, be normal.

Most of him didn't want to know, because it underscored his feeling of failure. When Tess had died, he had done everything wrong. And Amanda had done everything right.

It occurred to him he was thinking about Tess, allowing her name to cross his mind. Probably because of the picture of her on the mantel, and the clumsy wooden horse he had made with his own hands.

And yet, whatever the reason, he didn't feel like the very thought of her was going to shatter him like glass. And he had to admit that was new. A first.

Upstairs they passed an ajar door and he glanced in. Amanda's bedroom.

The kind of bedroom she had always deserved—a big four-poster bed, white eyelet cover on the bed, soft lights. The walls were painted solid light blue halfway up, and a band of oak wainscoting divided that from fresh-looking flowered wallpaper. It was a bedroom that hinted softly of sensuality, the mysteries of a woman's heart.

When they had been newly married they had a bed on an iron frame, two crates for end tables, and a couple of milk boxes stacked on top of each other for dressers. With a few yards of cheap cloth she had made drapes and a bedspread and covers for all the boxes.

She had turned something rough-and-tumble into something else, and he'd had the feeling she was doing the very same thing with him.

Of course, underneath the nice coverings it had still been a bunch of old junk.

She glanced back at him. He hoped he had managed to look straight ahead before she caught him peeking into her life, a starving man wanting scraps.

Had Doctor—what was his name? Sheep?—come up these steps with her? Shared that bed?

A stupid question. A none-of-his-business kind of question. And yet it burned in him, consumed him and he was still wondering when she quietly opened the door to the bedroom next to hers.

He was relieved to see it was not a child's room,

that she apparently had no immediate plans in that direction, even if she was seeing someone.

He wished, futilely, that the whole town wasn't so ghoulishly eager to keep him updated on Amanda. Did they do the same to her?

That would bore her near to death. *Saw Fletch in the grocery store today picking up a can of sardines and a jar of pickled jalapenos.*

The room was a home office and the child was sleeping on a bed folded out from a couch. Amanda's desk was stacked with various papers, two or three textbooks open on top of each other. There was a briefcase on the floor, another stack of papers beside that and a filing cabinet with an open drawer filled with more papers jutting out.

So, she worked after hours, too. Filling up the empty hours of her life, as he was, despite the doctor?

There was a computer and beside it, another picture of Tess. Her baby picture, the one taken at the hospital.

Happy birthday, sweetheart, wherever you are. I wish I could be with you.

The thought bushwhacked him, came out of nowhere. He could feel emotion clawing at his throat. That was the problem with allowing Tess into his mind. He turned swiftly from the picture, but not before he became aware of Amanda watching him.

With *knowing*.

He had to get out of there.

He went to the sleeping child and looked down at her face. Her hair had been taken out of the elastic and brushed. It was shiny, scattered around the delicate bones of her face. Her lips moved slightly, but she looked relaxed. She was clutching a little teddy bear.

That's why he had brought her here. Gauthiers' would never have supplied a teddy bear.

He told himself just to do his job, but almost of their own volition his fingers touched her cheek.

And jerked back, burned.

How he remembered the petal softness of a child's cheek.

Run for your life, he told himself.

He slipped a small pair of scissors from his breast pocket. He took just a smidgen of her hair from the tips where it wouldn't show and put it in a little Ziploc plastic bag.

He and Amanda went quietly back out the door. He knew his way now and found the steps fast. He went to the front door, not back to the kitchen.

"Thanks for supper." His voice sounded cold.

"You're welcome." So did hers. "I'll make a list of things she's going to need, even for a short stay." She handed him his jacket.

"Fine, I'll pick it up tomorrow." Which meant he had to come back tomorrow. No, he didn't. He could send Jenny. Anything to keep away from this big house on the hill.

"Fine," she said.

"Are you sleeping with him?" There it was out. Had just popped out on its own. His own mind bushwhacking him again.

"Who?" she said, innocently.

"Don't play with me, Amanda," he warned her darkly, heard his cop-conducting-an-interrogation tone too late to do anything about it.

Sparks, defiant, leaped in her eyes, but she answered. "No."

He let none of his relief show in his face. Instead he

said, "Well, maybe you should." And on that winning note, he opened the door, walked out and let it click firmly shut behind him.

But Amanda had never been one to let him have the last word. He heard the door open, her firm step on the porch. He glanced back. Her arms were folded over her chest and her eyes were blazing.

"Are you?" she asked. "Seeing anyone?"

Too much of a lady to ask if he was sleeping with anyone.

He snorted and got in the truck put it in gear and drove away, refusing to look back at her again. And refusing to ask himself what her interest might be, too.

He wasn't sure if his own small place had ever seemed quite as desperate or pathetic as it did that night when he went home.

And the river's song did not put him to sleep, as it usually did. Despite his exhaustion he lay awake.

He thought of the little girl. Was there a physical resemblance between her and him? Maybe her eyes were a similar color to his, but beyond that he couldn't see it.

It changed everything from a legal perspective, too. It was one thing to abandon a child, it was quite another to send her to her father.

He was a man who liked to deal with things only as they *needed* to be dealt with, and only after he had gathered all the facts and information he needed to make a decision. But still, he couldn't help pondering this one.

There was a hair of a possibility the child was his. What then?

In the morning, at the station, he asked Jenny to call Amanda and get the list of clothes the child needed.

"I might need you to take the little tyke shopping, too."

"No."

"Pardon?"

"No. It's not in my job description and I'm not doing it."

If she had a job description this was the first time he'd heard about it. He glared at her, knowing damn well what she was up to. Meddlesome old gal. Trying to get him and Amanda back together before things passed the point of no return with the doctor.

On the other hand, it had been his decision to leave the child with Amanda. Maybe it wasn't fair of him to expect others to carry the weight of his decision. But then, when had he ever been fair?

Still, Jenny was already back at work, studiously ignoring him, and he could tell by the set of her double chin she wasn't giving in.

And he wasn't going to give her the satisfaction of knowing it was any big deal to him. At lunchtime, he drove up the hill again. Partway up it occurred to him he could have probably gotten the list over the phone and catalogue ordered the stuff.

Of course, his mind insisted on telling him with a certain fiendish relish that there was the point-of-no-return thing.

And he'd found out last night the driveway was too narrow to turn around in halfway up.

Amanda and the girl were outside, the spring sunshine bright around them. The little girl rolled down the hill, and Amanda paused to watch her, a garden trowel in her hand. They both spotted him at the same time.

The little girl came running as soon as he parked the patrol car, like a puppy eager to have its ears scratched.

It wrenched his heart nearly out of his shirt.

So he picked her up and swung her around, even though that wrenched at his heart, too.

Amanda was coming now, in shorts, with her knees dirty and gardening gloves on the end of her hands. Her freckles were darkening even under the wide brim of her gardening hat.

At least he was wearing his uniform this morning. And had shaved. Not for her benefit, he told himself.

He set the girl down.

"Is she talking yet?" he asked Amanda, watching the child run after a butterfly.

She shook her head.

Suddenly the child was back in front of him. She had found a shell in the garden, and was pointing frantically at it, and then at herself.

"It's a seashell," he said, but she shook her head frantically, trying to tell him he wasn't getting it.

But Amanda did. "Shell? Your name is Shelly?"

The girl nodded then shook her head, began to run around them frantically, her arms outspread.

It was Amanda's turn to be stumped.

But he got it. "Shell. Bee. Shelby," he breathed, and then said it louder. "That's your name, isn't it? Shelby?"

The girl came back to him, her face wreathed in smiles.

"Hi, Shelby," he said softly.

"I'd like to have her hearing tested, see if there's any reason she can't speak," Amanda said. "Nothing official. A friend just agreed to look at her for me. Is that okay with you?"

It wasn't okay with him, even a little bit. The idea was okay, it was the friend part he didn't like. Because the whole town knew who her new friend was. He tried to tell himself she deserved a nice doctor. Rich. Well-educated. Well-adjusted.

Wimpy. Boring, his mind insisted on debating with itself.

"Oh, and here's the list of things she'll need. Bare essentials."

He concentrated hard on the list so that she wouldn't see the idea of her taking Shelby to her *friend* had flustered him beyond what the occasion warranted.

Two pairs of jeans. One pair of sweatpants. Three T-shirts. Two pairs of shorts. Barrettes. Pajamas.

He was beginning to feel out of his league entirely.

And then he saw the next item.

Five pairs of panties with pictures on them.

"I can order this stuff, right? From the catalogue?" He could actually feel heat burning up his cheeks.

"She needs it now. Catalogue orders can take a week."

"Oh."

"Is there a problem?" Amanda asked, ever so sweetly.

"As a matter of fact there is. I don't know anything about panties. With pictures on them? Jeez, Amanda. Five pairs. Why does she need so many?"

"Fletch! She needs fresh ones every day. Don't you?"

Oh, this was getting way out of hand. Now, they were going to discuss his underwear? Not while he lived, they weren't.

He shoved the list in his pocket. "I'll manage," he said tersely. He'd manage when he returned his cousin's truck. In another town. He was not going to have everyone in Windy Hollow talking about him buying panties. With pictures on them.

"We could go with you," Amanda said.

"Huh?"

"She'd probably love to pick out her own things. Look at those overalls. Do you suppose she's had anything brand-new in her life?"

He looked at Shelby, and didn't suppose she ever had. The T-shirt under the overalls was impossibly old and stained. It looked like something he might wear, off duty.

"Shelby, would you like that?" Amanda asked. "To go shopping and pick out some brand-new clothes?"

The little girl went very still, almost as if she could not believe what she had heard. She looked anxiously from one to the other, as if they might be playing a joke on her.

And then she nodded, one quick jerk of her head, as if the magic might go away if she agreed too strongly.

He wondered how this was happening to him. His whole life being wrested further and further out of his control. Control was a big factor in his life. It was the glue that held him together, even if at a deeper level he knew the truth. In those areas of life that really mattered, a man had no control at all.

He thought about just giving Amanda the money. But then he might be replaced with the doctor on the shopping trip.

Besides, he knew, looking at that little girl's face, that he wouldn't miss this opportunity to play Santa for the whole world.

"I guess you could come," he said with ill grace.

"Who knows? You might even have fun," Amanda said.

Fun. A word, a feeling, an action that had become completely foreign to him. He worked, he ate, he slept, he worked some more.

Somehow *fun* felt like it might be a threat to that measure of control he exerted over his life. But only women considered shopping fun, anyway. Women and possibly doctors.

Having thus convinced himself he was in no danger, he said, "I'll pick you up this afternoon. I have to bring my cousin's truck back to him. There's better stores in Belleview, anyway."

"That sounds fine," Amanda said serenely. "Doesn't it, Shelby?"

He saw the look on her face then, when she looked down at the little girl, and he felt something tighten in his heart.

Because it was so painfully evident to him that Amanda had retained her ability to care about things.

And he had not.

No wonder she had linked up with a doctor, a man who had made it his profession to care about life.

No wonder Fletch had stayed away from her for so long. Amanda was plain old bad for his heart. In a way no doctor could ever fix.

Chapter Four

When Fletch pulled back into Amanda's yard, he had once again switched to the black truck, but he was still in his uniform.

He leaped out of the truck, and Amanda remembered so well that energy that sang in the air around him. He'd always approached life with a certain urgency, as if he felt if he slowed down he might miss something.

The warm spring sun glanced off the badge and the midnight darkness of his hair.

She noticed the blue of his eyes as if she had never seen it before.

"I haven't had time to change and I have to come back to the office after, so if you don't mind, I'll go like this."

Amanda realized, when he said that, she must have been staring at him, and she quickly turned from him and began fussing with the snap on Shelby's overalls.

Somehow she had hoped he would change into something else.

From the very first time Amanda had seen him in that uniform she had known that Fletch had found the one thing that he was born to do.

Even dressed in blue jeans, a sweatshirt with the arms sawed off, a baseball cap on backwards, Fletch had always carried himself with an innate, and totally unconscious, aura of power. Under the ever present laughter in his eyes, even when he had only been nineteen, had been the easy confidence of a man who was completely assured in his own strength.

The uniform, the light-blue shirt, the winking gold badge, the knife-pressed navy-blue pants, the heavy black holster on his hip, and the pistol grip jutting from it, had accentuated that innate power, harnessed it.

In uniform, Fletch had been transformed before her eyes from a carefree boy to an intimidating man.

The uniform had—and did—make him look ten feet tall and bullet-proof.

And sexy as hell.

"It doesn't matter to me what you wear," she said, and hoped only she could hear the faint strangled note in her voice.

She suddenly wondered at her own choice of clothes—black shorts and spaghetti-strapped black top. She had told herself, as she put them on, that they would be cool and comfortable and casual, but now it seemed to her she had many outfits that would have been far cooler and far more comfortable and far more casual.

It was seeing him in that uniform again this morning that had made her choose this slightly naughty outfit over all her other choices. That uniform had always made her do crazy things.

She reminded herself, firmly, as she watched him

help Shelby into the truck, that Fletch had left her. She reminded herself, firmly, that her life was back on track and it was going to stay that way.

He moved back from the door and held it open for her. He seemed to notice, for the first time, what she was wearing and she saw a ripple of frank male appreciation in the still blue water of his eyes.

"I'm just going to go grab a sweater," she said.

He shot her an incredulous look. "It's a hundred and eight degrees in that cab and rising. No air-conditioning."

On the other hand, maybe it wouldn't hurt one little bit if he regretted what he had passed up.

Nose in the air, she brushed by him. His hand, where it held the door, brushed her naked shoulder. She felt the hardness of his knuckles and a shiver went through her that would have registered an even ten on the Richter scale, and she was not sure the Richter scale went that high.

She should have gotten the sweater.

"There's no apparent physical reason Shelby can't talk," Amanda told him, when he got in the other door, determined to keep the conversations impersonal, determined to remind herself Dr. Woodall Lamb was a part of her life now.

But the cab of the truck didn't smell of Woodall. She suddenly could not think if Woodall had a smell. Maybe, sometimes, he smelled faintly of medical soap.

No, the cab smelled of Fletch—a rich masculine aroma that did not come out of any bottle, and that was intensified by the heat.

She glanced over at him. The hard planes of his cheeks were already beginning to stubble with dark whiskers.

Without warning, Amanda remembered the scrape of those whiskers across her skin and felt a shiver that went to the bottom of her toes.

Mercifully, Shelby sat between them, bouncing with excitement, reaching out and touching his shoulder and then Amanda's as if she couldn't get enough of this kind of togetherness.

He nodded to acknowledge her comment about Shelby, but didn't say anything. He put the truck grimly in gear, clearly a man determined not to have *fun* if she had ever seen one.

A man, it occurred to her, determined not to look at her in that top. She stopped hugging herself.

"Did you say this is your cousin Brian's truck?"

"Yeah."

She saw this as a personal challenge, to see if she could squeeze a two or three-syllable reply out of Fletch. "How is he? Out of high school now, I imagine."

"He's okay."

Having achieved her first goal of three syllables, naturally she now wanted four or five. "Is he working?"

"Look, he drinks too much, and he drives too fast and can't hold a job."

"That's a cop's answer," she said, rolling her eyes.

"That's what I am."

Once, when she was young, that reply, with the hard edge around it, would have stopped her from asking any more questions. She saw, with unexpected clarity, that might have been part of the problem.

She had let him lead, unquestioningly. She had let him shut down conversations all those times he needed to talk the most.

"Can't you just say," she asked softly, "he's my favorite cousin, and I'm worried sick about him?"

Fletch gave her a black look, then retreated into silence.

She was not a young girl anymore who could be silenced with a look. She was a mature woman now, not content to let another take control. "Do you remember when you first applied for the job on the police force, how worried I was?"

He glanced at her, and she could tell he was uncomfortable, not knowing where this was going.

She was not all that certain herself.

"Do you remember that you laughed at my worry. You said, 'You can't seriously believe that being a cop in Windy Hollow is more dangerous than falling trees.'"

"How can you remember stuff like that?"

She shrugged. "I haven't decided myself if it's a gift or a curse." She was certain she remembered every word he had ever spoken. And also the way his hair had looked in the morning, that rooster tail sticking up in the back. The funny shape of his little toenail on his left foot. The way the bathroom smelled after he had showered.

"And the point is...?" he said gruffly.

"Being a cop was a lot more dangerous for you, Fletch." There it was out. And he was trapped in the truck with her. Finally, after all these years, they had to talk about it. Some of it. Some of the things that had gone wrong.

To what end? she asked herself desperately. And she answered herself that if there were parts of it not finished, she could not move on in the way she wanted to.

He was looking straight ahead. She could see that muscle in his jaw leaping. She couldn't force him to talk about it. But she could talk. All she wanted to. She was a mature woman with her own job and her own home, and she could talk about anything she damned well pleased.

She took a deep breath. Maybe the best place to start was at the beginning. "You remember Tommy Knutson, Fletch?"

He swore under his breath, and gave her a look that begged her to shut up. Begged. But she had shut up about it before.

"You did everything you could," she said. "You jumped into the river in February. You tried everything you knew how. You nearly killed yourself trying to save that boy."

"Why are you bringing this up?" he asked angrily. "That's—" he thought briefly "—more than eleven years ago."

She was willing to bet he knew the exact day and time. "Because that's the day I noticed you changing. Turning inward, not letting me come with you. And I let you. By my silence, I allowed you to believe your strength should have been greater. And I did it again and again. You handled things ugly and dangerous and draining, and you wouldn't talk about it, and I let you."

"Mandy, I'm from a family of loggers, for God's sake. I wasn't raised to talk about feelings. Men didn't do that."

"Some men do."

"Great. I hope you found one."

He said it easily, but she saw his knuckles were white on the steering wheel, and the pulse was beating in his throat. "I just wanted you to know how I felt about it."

"Eleven years later?"

"I should have said it a lot sooner."

"Are you teaching psychology or something at that college?" he asked suspiciously.

She laughed. "English."

"A support group!" he said triumphantly.

"No."

After a long time, he said, "I was trying to protect you. And Tess. I didn't want it to touch you."

"I know," she said simply. "We both did our best, but we were young, and we did some things wrong."

After a long time, he said, "You didn't do anything wrong, Mandy. I did. I know I did. But not you."

"A marriage is a partnership, Fletch. Even if you were the one who made every single mistake, I played a part. By being silent when I should have spoken up, by letting you think you had to be in charge of everything instead of telling you, 'Hey, I'm part of this team.'"

"I'm a lousy team player," he said, a confession he regretted because he added, quickly and lightly, "You should check out the psychology department. There are people who will pay to listen to stuff like that."

"A hint that you aren't one of them?"

He smiled at her, not angry anymore, relieved somehow, and she knew it was enough. For now.

Amanda focused on the little girl. She played car bingo with Shelby, on homemade cards she had prepared for the trip.

They had to find a cow, black and white, a red-roofed house, and three white cars to make a line. Then they'd start working on an X.

Shelby delighted in the game, pulling frantically on Amanda's arm when she saw one of the items.

"There's a house with a red roof," Fletch said suddenly. "Look way over there."

Then he seemed embarrassed that he had let on he was listening, even more embarrassed that he had participated. He glanced at her, and she didn't miss the heat in his eyes, before he looked away, quickly.

"I'll drop you two off at the mall, and go get my vehicle back from my cousin," he said.

She knew immediately why she wasn't going along for the car switch. He didn't want anyone in his family jumping to the conclusion they were back together. There was no point at all in asking him to say hello from her.

"Meet us in children's wear at the Mart," she said evenly and slammed the door.

The first thing she did was buy a too large white shirt, which she knotted over her black top. Thus protected from the heat in his eyes, she gave herself over to the fun of shopping with Shelby. It was painfully obvious the child had not had many shopping excursions. She touched the items Amanda found for her with soft fingers, her eyes round with wanting.

Together they loaded up a buggy with jeans, and sweatshirts, tops and sweaters.

Shelby was looking gleefully at a sweatshirt with Eeyore on it when Amanda glanced up and saw Fletch's long stride carrying him toward them. He looked wildly and hilariously uncomfortable in his uniform moving among all the pint-size racks.

A salesgirl appeared out of nowhere and planted herself in his route.

"Can I help you find something, sir?"

She was smiling with something just a little more than professional courtesy.

Well, this was a truth Amanda already knew. Women found Fletch irresistible. They had before he donned that uniform, and it seemed only to intensify his effect.

"No, thanks," he said, polite but curt.

The salesclerk looked disappointed and didn't move. Amanda watched as she leaned a little closer, whispered something to him.

Fletch turned red and walked by her as if she were invisible.

"What was that all about?" she asked him, raising an eyebrow.

"Nothing," he said sharply, and wandered away, pretending interest in the racks of clothing.

But Amanda knew. She had been coming out of the grocery store once when they were fairly newly married. Unaware she was there, Fletch had a young ruffian up against the side of his car, spread-eagle.

The woman in front of Amanda had turned to her with a conspiring smile and said, "He can frisk me anytime."

That night, worried, Amanda had mentioned that comment from a stranger to him.

He had laughed out loud. "Mandy Pandy, lots of women love a uniform. They don't know a thing about the guy inside it. The first time they saw me in my undershirt covered in grease from fixing the car, they'd run the other way. Not to mention if they saw the mess I leave in the bathtub."

And then softly, his forehead pressed to hers, his gaze unflinching on her face, he'd said, "Don't you get it, Mandy? You're my one and only, forever."

Then he'd pressed the worry lines from her forehead with his lips, and told her if she didn't stop it, he was going to have no choice but to take her into custody.

He'd waggled his eyebrows fiendishly at that, pulled his handcuffs from his back pocket and chased her around their tiny apartment until the neighbor below them had pounded on her roof—their floor—with a broom handle. Amanda had nearly died laughing.

Amanda cursed her memory. Photographic, but undisciplined. She ordered it to stop producing these pictures from the past.

But it didn't. She remembered the laughter fading, and her peeling the uniform off him, whispering to him fiercely she was wildly impressed with the guy inside that uniform, and then pressing her lips to the firm cut of his muscles, the silk of his skin.

With every ounce of her willpower she stopped the memory right there, made herself come back to the Children's Department, The Mart, Belleview, Montana.

She saw Fletch stop suddenly and glance around surreptitiously. Then he came toward them again.

In his hand was a hanger.

With a little white dress on it.

Wildly inappropriate. A fancy party dress, or a first communion dress, or a flower girl's dress. It had a white silky under layer, and then white frothy overlay, puffed sleeves, a wide white sash with a pink rose on it.

Amanda watched as Shelby spotted him coming toward them, and then froze in her tracks, her eyes glued to the dress. The Eeyore sweatshirt she had been holding slid out of her hands and formed a little puddle at her feet.

''Does this look like the right size?'' he asked, awkwardly holding out the dress.

''It looks perfect,'' she said firmly. Amanda didn't have the heart to tell him—or Shelby, either—the little dress wasn't even close to the kind of rough and tumble practical clothing they were shopping for.

There was a secret she knew about Fletch that no one else knew.

Under that exterior of icy control that women found so attractive, was something even more attractive. A tenderness of heart that Fletch tried so hard to hide. That he nearly destroyed himself trying to hide. That he would let it out, even in this small way, made her wonder if she might have made more progress in the truck than he had let on.

''Perfect,'' she repeated, then realized, aghast that she was looking up into his rough-hewn features, not at the dress at all. ''Shelby are you ready to try some things on?''

Hurriedly, she guided the little girl into the fitting room, leaving Fletch to glare at any salesgirl silly enough to approach him and ask what he needed.

Shelby insisted on skipping out of the small room to show him each outfit as she put it on, twirling in front of him.

At first he didn't have a clue what was expected of him. ''That's nice,'' he'd say awkwardly. ''That'll do, sure.''

The first time he told her she looked pretty, Shelby clapped with delight, and came back sighing with happiness.

He'd always been a quick learner.

Now he searched for adjectives to make the little girl beam. Gorgeous. Beautiful. Precious. Princess.

Finally, Amanda dropped the white dress over the child's head, and did up the sash. They both stared at her reflection in the mirror.

Shelby ran out the door to show Fletch, and Amanda trailed behind her.

She watched his face soften. He crouched down, and took those skinny shoulders between big hands, looked the child right in the eye.

"Shelby, are you sure you aren't a little angel come to visit us?" he asked, his voice gruff. Only someone who had loved him once would hear the emotion under that gruffness.

Shelby whirled and twirled and then raced back to him, threw her arms around his neck, and kissed him soundly on the cheek. Then she raced back to the dressing room giggling and flushed with pleasure.

But Amanda stood looking at him, transfixed, for just a moment longer, then before he noticed, turned and followed her little charge into the dressing room.

When she tried to get Shelby out of the dress, Shelby was having none of it. For a child without language she made it abundantly clear she was wearing the dress.

Fletch didn't seem to mind. In fact, he seemed to have no idea that it was not an everyday kind of dress.

On the way out, their basket loaded with far more clothing than they needed, they picked up socks and underwear, and it was Fletch who insisted everything have pictures on them.

Frogs frolicked across the socks, and flowers bloomed on the underwear.

When Amanda glanced at him, her breath left her body. She saw the faintest light shining in his eyes.

A light she had not seen for so long. Fletcher Harris was happy.

When they got to the cash register, she noticed he put everything on his credit card, except for the dress. He paid cash for that.

And then she understood. Everything else would be paid for by whoever paid for little lost children. But the dress was a gift from him. Which meant he knew it wasn't an everyday dress, after all.

"It seems like a dress like that should go somewhere," he said when they got into his vehicle, a brand-new SUV. "Should we go get a pizza?"

The different vehicle meant different seating arrangements. Amanda didn't have to debate very long. *She* was getting in the front. Shelby would sit in the back.

She told herself it was for safety, it had nothing at all to do with that memory of being chased around the apartment, the memory of the taste of his skin on her lips.

"Fletch," Amanda whispered, tucking Shelby into the back seat, doing up the seat belt around her, "that is not the kind of outfit you eat pizza in." He would never guess, not in a million years, that while she discussed dresses, her mind was focused only on him.

"Well, then let's take it back," he teased. "If you can't eat pizza in it, it's not worth having."

Amanda sighed, Shelby chortled and tried to let her know she wasn't getting pizza on her new dress.

They had been driving along for a few minutes when he touched her shoulder. She glanced at him and saw he was looking in the rearview mirror.

She glanced back at Shelby, who had her nose pressed against the window, a wistful expression on her face.

She was looking at a playground, teeming with children playing, laughing and running and squealing.

He was already pulling over. Was there any point telling him the dress wasn't up to this? Oh, what the hell. He'd bought the dress. He could worry about it.

"And look at that," he said, "a pizza place right across the street."

"I'll get the pizza," Amanda said, "you two go ahead."

She watched for a moment as they crossed to the park, hand in hand. Seeing him like that, with a small girl's hand held tightly in his own, his bigness in sharp contrast to Shelby's smallness, she felt a pang.

If they hadn't been so young, and had so much to learn... If Tess had lived...

But then, if she had learned a lesson from her pain, it was to appreciate what life gave her in this moment. To not spoil it by looking back and wishing or looking forward and guessing.

In this moment she had been given a little girl in a party dress discovering the world.

And for some reason, she had been given Fletch, for another moment in time. She could spoil those gifts entirely by thinking what might have been, by trying to look into the murky crystal ball of the future.

So, as she waited for the pizza, she watched them out the window. She smiled and it felt as if the smile went through to her soul. Underneath that gruff exterior, the muscled, pure-man menace, he was really just a big kid.

Amanda found herself laughing out loud as he tired of waiting at the bottom of the slide and climbed up the ladder himself. His legs in a V around Shelby, he swooshed down and then raced her to the ladder to do it again.

He pushed Shelby on the swing until it was going higher than it was ever meant to go, and then, somehow he was pushing all the kids on the swings, giving them under ducks. She could hear the shrieks and demands for *higher* all the way over here, through the open door of the pizza joint.

He soon had a whole circle of children around him, and he led them all to the merry-go-round, pushed it until it was whipping by, the children a blur of color and sound.

She could see young mothers looking up from their books, regarding him with indulgent smiles and interested eyes.

That was Fletch. No matter what he did, he always seemed to wind up at the center, rising to the top, attracting attention.

She took the pizza back across the street, and reluctantly Shelby waved to all her newfound friends and skipped over to her.

The dress was miraculously clean, as though, even while playing, Shelby guarded her new outfit.

The three of them sat on the grass in the shade of a huge maple. Fletch seemed so relaxed, some tension gone from his eyes, and from the way he held himself.

He laughed at Shelby's dramatic efforts not to get anything red on her dress.

It had been so long since Amanda had heard him laugh. She felt it weaken something in her. Wasn't it that bold, belly-deep laugh she had fallen for first?

She deliberately focused on Shelby, smiling to herself at the rapid rate in which three pieces of pizza disappeared into the tiny girl. Even focused so intently on Shelby, she noticed Fletch only ate one piece of pizza and wondered what had happened to that ferocious man-size appetite he had once had.

Shelby, licking the last of the sauce off her fingers, and after a careful and satisfied inspection of her dress, looked wistfully back at the children playing.

"Go on," Fletch said quietly. "Go play. You've worn me right out."

If Amanda had been worried about an awkward moment now that they were alone, she needn't have. He folded his hands under his head, laid back on the thick carpet of sweet-smelling grass and fell asleep almost instantly, the air slipping from him in gentle whispers.

It seemed to Amanda there was a trust factor involved in falling asleep so swiftly in front of someone else. Either that, or he was bored. But no, now that she could study him unobserved she could see there were circles of fatigue under his eyes. She acknowledged that she would have never noticed when his eyes were open, too busy drowning in the blue of them.

It was then, watching his face relaxed, the sweep of his thick lashes on his cheek, that the temptation began to play with her.

Taste him. Just one small kiss. On his cheek. He was snoring softly now, a man exhausted. He would never know.

A quick glance told her Shelby was totally involved with the other children, and the temptation grew.

Amanda studied the curve of his cheek, the squareness of his jaw, noticed, again, the dark crescents of tiredness under his eyes. She noticed, with him lying on his back, and his stomach caved in, that he had lost weight.

She knew he wouldn't be eating right. Forgetting to eat half the time. Eating out of cans and bags.

It was his vulnerability, rather than his strength, that finally made her give in.

She moved close to him. Touched the familiar silk of his hair with her fingertips. She studied him, the deep rise and fall of his chest, and convinced herself he slept deeply. That he would never know.

She brushed her lips over his cheek.

An awful truth hit Amanda. She had loved him always.

And she loved him still. Loving him and losing him had nearly killed her the first time, the final blow to a heart so racked in pain, it felt like it could not go on. She could not survive loving him again.

So when she bent over him again, and took his lips, she told herself she was really saying goodbye.

She remembered the taste of his lips. A taste of forests and raindrops, things strong and things mysterious. She remembered now, too, that even sleeping, he would answer the touch of her lips.

She had crept into their bedroom on tiptoe, sometimes, when he had come in from working the night shift and stolen kisses from him. He did now what he had done then.

In sleep his lips surrendering beneath hers, becoming soft and pliant.

She kissed him more deeply, knowing, telling herself this would be the last time.

And it was not until she broke away, that she realized his eyes were open, and he was watching her, desire and drowsiness side by side in the depths of ocean-blue eyes.

He didn't say goodbye.

Sleepily, he said, "Hello, Mandy Pandy."

She blushed like she had been caught without her bathing suit top on at a public beach. She looked everywhere but at him. She looked at the children playing, and her fingernails, and the tips of her toes.

He didn't make it any easier because he didn't say anything at all.

He didn't ask her why. He didn't move closer to her. When she dared glance at him, his eyes were closed, his chest rising and falling, deeply and evenly, again.

As if it had meant nothing at all to him.

Or maybe he really had slept through it.

She did what any woman in turmoil would do. She polished off the last three slices of pizza. And tried not to look at him again.

Chapter Five

God, he was tired. He felt as if he had not slept for days. Weeks. Years. As if his heart had waited for her, before it could relax, rest.

Amanda.

He thought he was dreaming of her kisses— warm, soft, sensuous, caressing his cheek, his lips. He relaxed. Finally home. Everything in his world finally right, and as it should be. Loved by Amanda.

But the sensation penetrated the gray cloud of weariness and suddenly he realized that it wasn't a dream.

It was real. Her lips, gentle, questing, on his.

He opened his eyes to further align himself with reality. Her eyes, the color of jade, half-closed, her hair soft and silky, falling forward and touching his cheek, tickling the side of his neck. He became aware that her breasts, soft and full, brushed his chest with the rise and fall of his every breath. Of its own accord, his breath quickened.

She realized suddenly that his eyes were open, that

her kiss had awakened him and she reared back, blushing and sweeping her fallen hair into place with her hand.

So, he had not lost his ability to make her blush. It reminded him of their first kisses—she the oh-so-good girl, not sure that she should.

Other firsts came into view. Their wedding night. Amanda, so shy, so sweet. So damned sexy. Far sexier than all those girls who tried so hard to be just that.

She was looking away, now, pretending it hadn't happened, that she hadn't stolen kisses from his lips. She looked incredibly flustered, and guilty, as if she'd been caught flashing or peeking in windows. If he said he was going to take her into custody, would she remember that game they used to play?

He longed to do what he had always done with her inhibition—to chase it away, to get to what breathed just underneath it. Wildfire. Passion.

He longed to put his hand to the back of her neck, pull her back down to him, lose himself in the spring wine of her kisses.

He closed his eyes against the pain of loneliness he suddenly felt—so aware of how bereft his life was without her. His sun gone. His reason to exist.

If he kissed her again, he could pretend that was not so.

For a moment or two.

And maybe that moment or two would have enough warmth in it to keep his heart from the cold for a day, or a month, or a year. Or maybe it would just break into a million pieces all over again. He marshaled his strength. Not to take her in his arms and kiss the living daylights out of her. Kiss her until the passion exploded between them. Kiss her until she was breathless and couldn't think.

And wouldn't remember. How he had let her down when she needed him most. How he had not been the man she needed him to be, or the man he needed himself to be.

The problem was, even if she could forget, he couldn't.

And some things were beyond forgiveness.

But then it was as if she spoke those words, all over again, that she had said in the truck. *We both did our best, but we were young, and we did some things wrong.* He sat up abruptly. He was not an introspective man. He was a man of action. And right now that action should be to put as much distance between him and her as he could—a problem since he had to get her back to Windy Hollow.

He brushed grass off the back of his shirt and wondered where that white shirt Amanda was wearing had come from. She hadn't been wearing it when he picked her up this morning. No, she'd been in a skimpy black outfit that didn't look like anything he thought a schoolmarm should wear. And she had a purse the size of a wallet slung on a black string around her shoulder. The new cover-up hadn't come out of there.

He'd probably been looking at her with unleashed lust.

So she'd very sensibly bought something to cover up with. She was trying to protect herself from him. Good idea.

Then why the hell had she kissed him? Because that's what she was, and always had been. Contradictions. Most sensible. Most sensuous. Most predictable.

And most unpredictable at the very same time. Doctor's daughter. Blue-collar worker's wife.

Let's face it. He had known he was playing with fire from the minute he'd given in to the temptation to go up her driveway with that little girl asleep beside him in his truck.

Now he had to save them both. Take her home, keep it professional. No more outings, eating pizza, shopping for little girl's dresses. It was insanity to tangle with this *stuff*.

Stuff being all the messy things inside himself that he'd never really been able to understand, stuff stored in locked places, along with tears and feelings and weakness of any kind. Stuff being a brand-new awareness of the four-year-old ache in his heart.

"We have to go. I have work to do," he said. He heard the stiffness in his own voice. The coldness. Protective. To keep her from knowing what she could do to him in just seconds.

Amanda wouldn't look at him.

So, maybe he did things to her, too.

Of course, he could ask her, *Why did you do that? Why did you kiss me?* He could try doing something different, talk about how he felt, about this great well of confusion inside of him.

But what he felt was clouded by the fact he could still taste her on his mouth. And as much as he wanted to, he could not bring himself to wipe the taste away.

Before he had a chance to frame what he wanted to say—to answer his father who was staring at him from across the years, telling him Harris men didn't talk, they acted—she got up and brushed imaginary grass off the seat of her shorts.

"Shelby!" She was moving toward the park. "It's time to go, sweetie."

He watched them coming back toward them, hand in hand. For a moment it felt as if he couldn't breathe.

This was what his life might have been.

If.

That word was destroying him. *If* they hadn't taken Tess to day care that day. *If* he had taken the day off work. *If* he had, by some chance, dropped by the day care just as it was happening. *If* he had been the one to answer the emergency call. Oh, he knew the first responders had done everything humanly possible. But he harbored this belief that he would have done *more* than what was humanly possible. *If* he had been there, maybe the miracle would have happened for him.

And then there were the *ifs* that came after a pint-size white coffin and a waxen-faced child was buried with her teddy bear in her arms.

He had tucked her red coat in beside her, stupidly mumbling to Amanda *in case she gets cold.*

More *ifs.* *If* he hadn't handled his grief by trying to be so damned strong for Amanda, collapsing finally under the weight of his unspoken despair. He'd dived into a bottle and stayed there, lost, for two years.

Two years. Amanda had put up with it a lot longer than she should have. He'd walked away from her for her own good. She hadn't known that then, but she probably did by now.

What *if* he had been able to talk to her, what *if* he had been able to break his self-imposed prison of silence and strength as she had suggested in the truck on the way over here? Could it have been a happy ending if he had ever learned to rely on someone other than himself?

Just another big *if.*

If he'd been able to talk to her, to tell her, Mandy, I'm so afraid. He'd never been afraid before, but after Tess died, he lived with fear night and day.

His fear was that the God who had not listened to his prayers for his daughter's well-being would take Amanda from him, too.

Lost in hurt, in fear, in self-loathing, he'd abandoned Amanda, figuring she was way better off without him.

If he hadn't have done that, maybe they could have fixed things. Maybe, eventually there would have been another child. And then maybe this could have been their real life—woman and child walking toward him, hand in hand, the sun shamed by their radiance.

So many *ifs.*

But he could not stay imprisoned by those two tiny letters. He knew they were a trap that would lure him back into the pit of despair.

He forced himself to take a deep breath. To focus on the warmth in the air, the scent of it, the lively new green of the grass. To focus on the birds singing and the delighted screams of the children floating across from the park.

Finally, he was able to look at them again. He forced himself to focus only on Shelby and her mystery. Something he could deal with. Something he could do something about. Solve. Analyze. Fix.

He looked intently at the child. The dress had a big smudge on the front of it. He had known the dress wasn't made for playing in the park. But he also knew what it was to be the kid who never owned one thing nice or one thing new.

And what it was like to have someone see beyond that rough exterior to see who you really were in your soul, to have that person believe you were good and special.

For him that person had been Amanda, who had seen him, who had looked beyond the rough edges, the wildness. Had he always been the man she thought he was? Or had her faith in him made him more than he had ever been before?

Shelby's smile grew as she came closer to him. He was not sure what he had done to deserve her delight in him, her trust in him.

And then she glanced down at her dress, and her smile faltered. She stopped in her tracks, stared at the smudge and then looked anxiously to him, and then to Amanda.

She began to cry.

And suddenly who he had been four years ago, or ten years ago, or even last week, didn't matter.

All that mattered was the man he could be in this moment.

He strode over to Shelby and lifted her chin. "It doesn't matter," he told her, as gently as he could. "It's only a dress."

But she shook her head, tears flying, not accepting his forgiveness. She brushed at the dirt on the front of her dress with frantic fingers.

His hand closed over her fingers.

"Sweetheart, what matters is what's inside that dress, not what's on the outside of it." He lifted her up, felt her arms go around his neck, and her legs wrap around his waist. Her tears rolled inside his shirt collar.

And it occurred to him, maybe starting so young, people got in the terrible habit of being way too hard on themselves. They put themselves in a position where they couldn't forgive what others forgave them in an instant.

He looked at Amanda. She was watching him, some soft tenderness in her eyes—just the way she had looked a long time ago when he held Tess.

He closed his eyes. And when he opened them, he was determined to look forward instead of back. He smiled at Amanda, cautiously.

She looked hastily away. But not before he caught the faintest glimmer of something in her eyes. Hope.

And all his doubt slammed back into him. He was not the kind of man who should be offering people hope.

In the vehicle on the way home, he let Amanda handle the conversation department. But soon, given Shelby's silence from the back seat and the abruptness of his own monosyllabic replies, she became discouraged and gave up on talking.

"Would you like me to sing, Shelby?" she asked. "I know some great songs."

No, please, anything but that. She didn't have a good singing voice. It was scratchy, and her efforts to hit the higher notes were downright painful. But her enthusiasm made up for her lack of skill.

A jagged-edged memory came flooding back: coming in late from a shift and finding Amanda in the nursery, crooning to the baby. Kids' songs and folk songs, and songs that she made up as she went along. Love songs.

"'We're having a purple stew,'" Amanda sang out, impervious to his memories.

How could she not be self-conscious around him, when he felt as if he were tied up in knots around her? When he felt as if he had to calculate every move in

terms of its repercussions, and how it might be inter-
preted?

"'With purple tomatoes, and purple potatoes and
you!'"

He glanced at her. Somehow the enthusiasm that was
in her voice was not in her eyes. So maybe she was
doing the very same thing as him. Finding safe ground.
Singing silly songs was so much safer than talking
about the past, their mutual friends, members of the
family they had once shared, *feelings*.

Their regrets.

"Stooby-dooby-dooby-doo."

And suddenly over the sound of Amanda's, he heard
another sound. He listened intently. Shelby was humming. When she saw him looking at her in the rearview
mirror she stopped, abruptly.

So, he began to sing, too.

"'Purple potatoes and purple tomatoes and *you*'."
He hated singing. His had not been a family of music.
They had scorned the finer things. There had always
been chain saws in the kitchen. They ate with their
fingers. His mother and father had sworn with equal
experience and gusto.

As a young man, Fletch had come to Amanda wondering what she would ever see in him.

And with a little worm of doubt in the pit of his
stomach that he would never, ever be good enough for
her.

He sang louder. He had to hand it to Amanda. Singing was a pretty good technique for distancing from
discomfort.

Amanda looked at him astonished, missed a beat,
caught his quick backward glance and began to sing,
louder.

He forgot he didn't like singing.

He was amazed how he knew all the words. "Purple Stew" ended. They started on "The Ants Go Marching."

Sure enough, the louder he sang, the louder his small passenger hummed, confident her small noises were being lost among the larger ones.

He was bellowing "'The ants go marching three by three, hurrah, hurrah.'"

He strained to hear above his own racket.

There it was. A little tiny hum, not much more than the vibration of his pager in his pocket.

"'The littlest one stopped to—'" Amanda said, "'scratch a flea,'" and he said, "'to take a pee,'" and Shelby laughed.

Out loud.

Amanda and he exchanged a glance and kept on singing. They sang every song they knew, and sometimes, he was sure he could hear a small whispered voice joining theirs.

At fifty-two bottles of beer on the wall, Shelby fell asleep.

"She was singing," Amanda said quietly, glancing back at her.

"I know," he said cautiously, focusing on the child in his rearview mirror. Shelby's chest rose and fell, her chin dropped.

"Now what?"

The cop in him wanted to push. To unlock the secret to getting the little girl to talk. The cop wanted solutions.

But the man in him answered, "Let's just be patient. Let it unfold. Let her talk to us, when she's ready. Meanwhile, lots of singing."

"You never used to be patient," Amanda said. She laughed. "Or a singer."

"I'm not the same person I was." He said it coldly, his No Trespassing signs high and wide. She ignored them.

She never used to ignore them. She used to respect it when he didn't want to talk about things.

"Do you mean that in a good way or a bad way?" She pressed. "That you aren't the same person that you were?"

He sighed, annoyed, and yet somehow relieved, too, that she just wasn't giving in to him. "I have no idea," he admitted.

She laughed, again, softly.

"What about you, Mandy? Are you better or worse?" He left the rest unsaid. *Since our baby died. Since we aren't together anymore.*

"I'm not better or worse, Fletch, just different. Altered. Deeper, maybe. Wiser."

The silence drifted between them. He begged himself not to ask. Begged. And yet, there were the words, tumbling out of his mouth. "Are you in love with that doctor everybody keeps telling me you're seeing?"

"Oh, Fletch."

"It's kind of a yes-or-no answer."

"How about a none-of-your-business answer?"

He felt a deep stirring of satisfaction. She didn't love the doctor.

His satisfaction lived for about five seconds.

"I'm not looking for excitement, anymore, Fletch. That's a young person's game. I'm looking for contentment. Someone to throw an afghan over me when I fall asleep watching TV. Someone to watch the bird feeder with, and say 'Oh, there's the yellow-bellied sapsucker.' Someone who'll bring in a load of wood, and look after the car, and help me refinish old furniture.''

He stared straight ahead. That was one thing he couldn't give her. Contentment. As if either of them had ever fallen asleep watching TV. Had they watched TV? No. They chased each other around the house, screaming with laughter, and fell asleep in each other's arms on the living room rug afterward.

She wanted to watch birds?

Why did he feel so angry? She wanted someone to share her life, to carry some of the burden. That was normal. That was natural. So what?

She was settling for less than she deserved, that was what.

Settling for the earth when she could have the stars.

Settling for mediocrity when she could have ecstasy.

Settling for contentment instead of bliss, for plain old garden variety yellow-bellied sapsuckers instead of birds of color and glory like pheasants and peacocks.

And whatever feelings he had left for her, he could not allow her to do that. To hell with being professional.

Slowly, deliberately he pulled over onto the shoulder and shut off the engine. The only sound in the vehicle was the soft, even sound of Shelby snoring.

''Is something wrong?'' Her eyes were wide on him.

''Yeah.'' He undid his seat belt, with barely a glance at her.

''What? A flat tire? Something wrong with the engine?''

Without answering, he slid out of his seat and got out his door. Aware of her eyes following him, puzzled and wary, he went around the front of the vehicle, opened her door, and stepped back.

"Get out," he snapped, all cop, not wanting to brook any nonsense from her.

She gave him a startled look, started to say something, looked at his face, and unsnapped her seat belt. She stepped out of the vehicle, took an uncertain step back from him.

Deliberately, never taking his eyes off of her, he closed her door.

"Fletch?" she said, worried.

He leaned toward her. If he was not mistaken, she leaned toward him, too. He saw it register in her eyes that she knew, the instant before his lips touched hers, what he was going to do.

Knew and froze like a deer caught in headlights.

Helpless against this thing between them.

He tasted her lips with slow and fierce possessiveness. It was not the kind of kiss she had given him. It was not innocent and sweet and soft and secretive. It was hard, and hungry, and demanding. It was honest. It was everything he felt and had tried so desperately to hide.

For just a second, she froze. She inched her hands up between them and pushed, but he sensed the lack of conviction, and instead of retreating from the pressure of her hands, he pushed hard against it, trapping her hands between them.

When he slid his hands behind the small of her back and pulled, she surrendered against him, pliant. Her lips opened beneath his.

He accepted the invitation and plunged his tongue into the cool hollow of her mouth. She tasted of rain and mist.

How could such contact kindle such heat?

It was one of those miracles of a man and a woman, that the moist fullness of lips touching, tongues exploring, could ignite. Sparks. Shuddering through him. And her.

Her pliancy was gone, now, replaced by her body meeting his, melding with it, so close he could feel the softness of her nipples suddenly harden.

Sparks became flame, tentative, reaching skyward, intertwining, dancing, fading, leaping again.

He nursed the flame deliberately. He knew all about starting fires. Too much force or too much fuel now would put it out.

And so he softly separated his lips from hers, and she moaned. The moan hadn't yet died in her throat when he began to explore the tenderness of her eyelids, her earlobes, and the hollow of her throat with his fevered lips. He kissed her temples and the tip of her nose, and then dropped his mouth to the bare, silky expanse of skin above the primly buttoned V of her newly purchased blouse.

Fire leaped and crackled and burned and glowed.

He knew fire. It would take care of itself, now. Feed itself. Know without coaxing where to go next, what to do next. He knew fire. It would leap higher and stronger and wilder until it devoured the past and the future and the pain.

Oh, how he had missed her. Had missed the taste of her, the sweetness of her mouth, the temptations of her tongue, the soft swell of her breasts meeting the unyielding line of his chest, his thigh nudging between hers.

He was never going to let her go. Never.

He was going to lay her down in the grass—

Peripherally, he heard the rumble of approaching tires on the pavement. Peripherally he registered he could not possibly lay Amanda down in the grass beside a public roadway, while he was in uniform. While a child in their charge slept on. The thoughts sprinkled icy cold water on the flame.

The blast of the horn, long and loud and intrusive, doused the rest of it.

He broke his mouth away from Amanda's, glanced toward the road in time to see Thelma's black Mustang whizzing past them.

Amanda gasped, shoved at him hard with both her hands, and meant it this time. She broke his hold on her, and stepped back, glaring at him and panting.

"How dare you!" she said. Her voice was angry, but her eyes were hungry.

Her stuck-up-scholar voice might have made him smile under different circumstances. "Double dare me," he said. "I'll do it again."

"Why?" she asked, wiping frantically at her lips, as if she could make herself believe she hadn't participated.

"You started it," he said, folding his arms over his chest.

"I did not."

"Oh? What would you call that back there in the park?"

"Nothing. I—I was saying goodbye! What were you doing?"

He felt the knife edge, razor sharp, posed right over his chest. *She was saying goodbye.*

"I could have sworn you said that already. Four years ago."

"It seems to me you were the one who said it."

Standing here fighting with her over things long dead and long gone beside a public roadway was not much better than kissing her beside it. "I was doing you a favor," he said quietly. "That's why I kissed you. To make bloody sure that you won't ever be happy with contentment. Security. Watching yellow-bellied sapsuckers, and refinishing old junk." He snorted. "Amanda Cooper looking for contentment. I should take you into custody."

The memory flared in her eyes, and then went out as surely as the fire between them just had. Her voice sounded oddly old. "I told you, I've changed."

"Yeah, you did tell me that. And you know what that kiss told me?"

She wouldn't ask. She took a sudden interest in her feet, and then in the semi that roared by them. It tooted its horn, too.

He took a step closer to her, and she looked up, just as he had known she would. "That told me you haven't changed one little bit. Under that cool, haughty Miss Priss exterior, you're still on fire."

"I am not!" As an afterthought, she added, "And I do not have a Miss Priss exterior. Or interior! I am not prissy!"

She was flustered, though, and he was satisfied with that. He shrugged, moved around the front of the vehicle, got back in. He leaned over and opened her door. She hesitated before she got back in.

"Don't touch me again," she warned in a voice that suggested she had taken karate and would give him a punch to the throat if he did.

"Don't worry, I won't. I think I made my point." He started the engine, pulled out. The child slept on.

"This has always been the problem," she said.

"What has always been the problem?"

"*You* deciding you know what's best for me."

He had thought the problem was that their baby died. He hated it that she thought it went deeper than that. Hated it.

The strained, angry silence lasted right to the outskirts of Windy Hollow.

"Who was that who drove by us and honked?" she asked, not quite managing to sound as if she didn't care.

"Just now?" he asked innocently.

"No. Back there!"

He liked that. That at the moment that horn had blasted them both back into reality, she'd been too dazed to take notice of who it was driving by them. He probably would have missed it, too, except for the fact that a cop never missed a detail.

"Thelma," he said.

"Thelma Theobald?" she asked, unable to contain her horror.

"One and the same," he said, not without satisfaction.

"Thelma Theobald," she repeated wearily.

He watched out of the corner of his eye, as she studied her fingernails. "That's right," he said, without an ounce of sympathy. "It'll be all over town by tomorrow."

"Fletcher?"

"Hmm?"

"Please don't. Please don't ruin my life."

Her voice was small and broken, and suddenly he felt ashamed of himself. He couldn't give her what she needed. He had failed her. They both already knew that. What kind of small-minded man would get in the way of her getting on with her life?

He knew she had this effect on him. He knew it. That's why he'd been crossing streets and turning U-turns in the middle of downtown to avoid being anywhere near her.

He knew he wasn't good for her. And that when he was around her, he was powerless over the helpless desire he felt, the passion, the quickening of his pulse and the crying of his heart. If there was one thing Fletch Harris scorned it was powerlessness.

"All right," he heard himself, agreeing, but it cost him, cost him plenty. Maybe even everything he had left.

Had some small sliver of hope survived within him?

Chapter Six

Amanda sat on her porch swing and gazed out at her yard. She was not sure when she had seen a morning so intensely beautiful. Her early spring flowers were nearly finished, but this morning, the tulips and hyacinths and daffodils had been returned to glory, beaded with drops the shapes of tiny tears. The grass was blanketed with flashing diamonds of dew, as well, and small sneaker prints were part of the delightful pattern.

Shelby, peacock proud in her new sweatpants and T-shirt, was out with a basket, snipping blossoms carefully—a gift for Fletcher's grandmother whom she would be spending the day with. The sun played on her hair, on the roundness of her cheeks, and on the lines of her arms.

Amanda wondered how much that kiss a few days ago on the side of the road had to do with this way she was looking at the world—with wonder. With a kind of bubbling exhilaration.

Woodall pulled up the driveway in his white, four-door sedan. It struck her, foolishly, that it looked like an old man's car. She reminded herself that she had ridden in it many times without feeling that at all.

She had ridden in it and thoroughly enjoyed the luxury of deep leather burgundy seats, music pouring around her, feeling safe and secure riding in such a well-maintained, reliable vehicle with such a sensible, calm driver at the wheel. He seemed to have none of Fletch's urgency to get places fast.

Woodall got out of the car and carefully closed the door. No slamming. He gave the mirror an affectionate little pat, and then turned and came up her walk.

He was a nice-looking man. He was not tall or muscular like Fletch and he had none of that rugged outdoor appeal that was Fletch's. On the other hand, women wouldn't ever make indecent proposals to him in the Children's Wear department of the Mart. She gave herself a shake.

Was everything in her whole world going to be compared to Fletch now? That's how it had been for far too long. Every man who showed the faintest interest in her had been compared and found wanting. Amanda had thought, with Woodall's arrival in her life, she had finally moved beyond that.

Woodall was solidly, wonderfully average. He had distinguished, prematurely gray hair. It was thinning just a touch at the crown, and he endearingly arranged strands over the bald spot. He was medium height with a boyish build and a youthful face. She had always liked his eyes—his gaze steady, his brown eyes so kind. Even dressed casually, he always looked classy—a man who would fit in anywhere.

Today he was wearing pleated cream trousers, a knife-edged crease down the center of each leg and a dark-brown shirt embossed delicately over the pocket with the emblem of the Windy Hollow Golf and Country Club.

She wondered if Fletch had ever worn cream-colored trousers, and the thought made her smile.

His off duty wardrobe then was limited to blue jeans. The more holes in them the more he had liked them. Was it the same, now? Probably worse, without someone to occasionally weed through the worst of the jeans, put the ones with only white threads left on the fanny surreptitiously out in the trash.

She gave her head another shake. Fletch was not going to spend the day with her and Woodall! She vowed she would not think of him again.

She rose to greet Woodall, aware what a good match she made for him, in her cream slacks, and the matching blouse with the faint brown line in it. Nothing even remotely naughty about this outfit. He came up the stairs and took both her hands, giving her an affectionate buss on the cheek.

She would not compare that to the kiss from a few days ago. She would not! But even the fact that the kiss had flashed through her mind meant she had kept her vow not to think of Fletch for less than thirty seconds.

"You look lovely, as always." Woodall beamed. "Are you ready? The antique auction in Thompson Falls starts at ten. And I heard about a wonderful new bed-and-breakfast over that way that serves lunch in their back garden. Very Victorian. I booked us a table."

Had Fletch succeeded, then? Once, this simple plan for the day would have filled her with contentment. Now, she felt vaguely restless.

"That sounds, um—" *utterly boring* "—lovely," she said. "Shelby."

The little girl danced out from the back of the house, her basket full to overflowing with flowers. She stopped when she saw Woodall, scratched the back of her leg with the toe of her other foot, and looked shyly at the ground.

"Is she coming with us?"

Amanda cast Woodall a glance. An option that obviously distressed him, though he was doing his best not to show it.

"No, we're going to drop her off at Teresa Harris's house."

The look of relief that crossed his face was short-lived. "Harris," he said. "And that would be what relation to you?"

"She's my ex-husband's grandmother."

He obviously wanted to say something more, but to her relief, thought better of it. "Well, let's go, shall we?"

Was there a tightness around Woodall's mouth that she had never seen before? No, he was smiling warmly at Shelby, admiring her flowers. He opened the back door for her, and helped her fasten the seat belt. He cautioned her to be careful with the flowers, then ran around to get Amanda's door.

He opened it with flourish and gave her a little bow.

He was not pretentious. He was not. Oh, she was going to kill Fletch Harris next time she saw him. For doing this to her world.

She settled in the seat, and he came around to his.

"New CD," he said happily. "Listen. Tchaikovsky."

"I thought he was dead," she said as the first heavy notes of the music filled the car.

Woodall laughed indulgently. "Of course, he's dead. But good music never dies. This recording is by the London Symphony."

She glanced over her shoulder. Shelby had her fingers in her ears.

Amanda acknowledged, sadly, she really didn't deserve this man. For all that she came from a well-heeled family, she was a cretin. Her tastes ran to, well, "Purple Stew."

"Turn right here."

In just a few moments, they were in front of Fletch's grandmother's house. The yard was huge, the house was small. But everything was so tidy and appealing. Shutters freshly painted, flower borders freshly turned, shrubs trimmed, grass manicured.

Obviously, at eighty-one, Teresa was no longer doing this kind of work herself. The house and yard looked better than they ever had, which probably meant the old woman was being a terrible taskmaker to Fletch.

"You don't mind if I just wait?" Woodall asked, and without waiting for her answer leaned back in rapture, his right hand holding an imaginary baton as he directed the London Symphony.

"Not at all."

Amanda collected Shelby and the basket of flowers, and went up the walk. Memories. Of coming here for Sunday dinner and neighborhood picnics on the grass. Of the happiness in Teresa's weathered old face when Tess would toddle up that walk toward her.

"Hello, love."

Amanda glanced up. Teresa was waiting in the shade

of the porch, and she rose now and came down the steps, her eyes twinkling on Shelby. She was tall, like Fletch, but age was making her gaunt. Her gray hair was short, her print dress covered with a huge white apron.

Of course, she and Amanda saw each other from time to time. If they ran into each other downtown they went for tea together. Teresa had brought her cuttings for her garden when she had moved into her new house. Amanda always called her on her birthday, sent flowers on Mother's Day, took great care in selecting just the right Christmas gift for her every year.

But, by unspoken agreement, Teresa belonged to Fletch, as if the two women both knew he was the one who needed her more. She would anchor him to his sanity when all else failed. The old house and the old woman would provide enough work to keep his muscles aching, to turn his focus, even briefly, away from a broken heart.

And both of them had known if Amanda came here, continued her relationship with Teresa, that he would not.

The two women embraced long and hard, and then Teresa took a step back and put her hands on both sides of Amanda's face.

Her hands felt wonderful. The skin papery and soft, but the strength still there, the spirit lively in her eyes.

"You look beautiful," Teresa decided approvingly.

"Thank you. So do you."

Teresa snorted, but was obviously pleased. "And this must be Shelby. That rascal of a grandson of mine told me all about you."

Shelby's eyes went very round when she realized it was Fletch being called a rascal. Or maybe she thought

of grandsons as being her own age. Shyly, she handed
Teresa the basket.

"Shelby, this is Fletch's grandmother, Teresa Harris."

"You can call me Baba."

"She doesn't talk," Amanda said quietly.

"Of course she talks," Teresa said firmly. "She just
needs the right person to talk to, and that person will
probably be me." She buried her face in the basket,
fussed over each blossom and named the plant that had
produced it. When she lifted her face, she looked over
Amanda's shoulder for a moment.

"What a lovely car," she said. "Is that the new
beau?"

Amanda looked quickly over her shoulder. Woodall
looked like he was swatting flies, flailing away now
with both hands, his left keeping the beat, his right
sweeping the air in front of him.

"Er, that's him."

Teresa gave her a long look that said quite a bit more
than if she had spoken, then turned her attention to
Shelby.

"Come now," Teresa said, putting the basket in one
hand and holding out her other. "We've got much to
do today. Fletch will be here soon, and he likes those
sugar cookies. They're out of the oven, but they
haven't been decorated yet, and you look like a girl
who knows how to decorate sugar cookies. Are you?"

Shelby nodded, a bit uncertainly, and placed her
hand in the elderly lady's.

"I knew it!" Teresa said. "Could tell just looking
at you. Could tell you liked to garden, too. I picked
out some flowers for just you to put in today. Do you
like petunias?"

Shelby nodded solemnly, though Amanda was pretty sure she wouldn't know a petunia from a marigold.

"And, of course, I have a marvelous new CD. The Drovers sing, 'When I Was Three Foot Three.' Have you heard it?"

Shelby shook her head, side to side, no.

"Amanda, have a lovely day. Now, how does it go? Oh, yes, like this. 'When I was three foot three, and everyone was bigger than me...'" They turned and went down the walk together.

Teresa looked back, and winked, but Shelby skipped ahead, practically dragging Teresa up the front steps.

With a sigh of relief that Shelby and Teresa were obviously well-matched, Amanda turned back to Woodall.

He was still lost in the music, leaning back, his eyes closed, directing the London Symphony with great and enthusiastic flourish, his head now moving so vigorously that the hair he combed so carefully over the bald spot had sprung free.

Amanda prayed Fletch wouldn't show up now. As she opened the door and slid in, she felt sudden regret.

That she was not going to spend the day making sugar cookies and gardening and listening to the Drovers.

Woodall opened one eye and looked at her, then sat up and started the ignition. He took a quick look in the mirror, smoothed his hair back into place and announced, "Thompson Falls here we come," he said, as if they were going to Vienna or Paris.

"Here we come," she said, and smiled weakly at him.

As they were about to pull away, Fletch's vehicle careened around the corner. He was coming from the opposite way and skidded to a halt across from his grandmothers. He got out and slammed the door, hard.

"No way to treat that vehicle," Woodall muttered disapprovingly. He put on his signal light and pulled carefully onto the empty street.

She tried to look straight ahead. So how was it she knew Fletch was wearing jeans faded nearly white, and a sweatshirt with no arms that said Windy Hollow Bull Dogs on it?

That showed off every leaping muscle in his arms.

That made her remember what it was to be in those arms just a few short days ago.

"Is that him?" Woodall asked, watching in his rear-view mirror as Fletch passed behind the back of the car. He frowned slightly.

"Who?" she asked.

He cast her a glance. "Your ex-husband."

"Oh. Yes. That's him."

"My God. Man-made mountain."

Somehow he managed to say it as if all that size and strength was a bad thing.

"Now," he said, changing the subject as smoothly as he drove, "anything special we're looking for today?"

"I was thinking of a chest," she said, and then felt the heat growing up her cheeks. Because she was thinking of a chest. Fletch's chest, broad and strong, carved from bronze.

"A Shaker piece would be nice," she said hastily. "Or early pioneer pine. That corner in the dining room needs something."

"So," Woodall said, delighted, "a morning spent looking at chests."

Somehow, she knew if Fletcher ever said they were

going to spend the morning looking at chests, he would mean something quite different. He'd have that smoky look in his eyes and that wicked grin on his face.

Woodall turned up the music and started directing again, waving his right hand enthusiastically and humming.

Amanda sighed and looked out the window.

At the auction her attention wandered. There were two nice chests there, but somehow they didn't interest her. Instead, she found herself looking longingly at an antique porcelain doll and a baby carriage.

The wrong kind of toys for Shelby, entirely. Toys that were meant to be looked at instead of played with.

The back garden where Woodall took her for lunch was delightful: a quiet flagstone patio, finely wrought cast iron furniture, a small pond, a showy spring garden. They ate tiny finger sandwiches, and sipped tea from Royal Doulton china. They finished with a selection of delicate pastries and a crystal bowl of fresh strawberries.

Woodall talked about the bronze spittoon he had picked up for his office. Somehow, she couldn't share his enthusiasm for a container designed to spit disgustingly used tobacco into, and that had actually been used for that purpose once upon a time. Even though it was meticulously clean, Amanda found the spittoon vaguely revolting.

Her mind drifted back to Windy Hollow. She wondered what they were doing now. She imagined Fletch and Shelby kneeling side by side, pressing the dirt intently around some new seedling.

Woodall's hand covered hers, and she started.

"You're not quite here today," he noted mildly. "I thought you'd snap up that chest."

She wished he'd quit talking about chests, especially since his was the last one she'd want to snap up. It felt like a betrayal even to think that. They were becoming such good friends, the future looked so promising. She knew he was going to ask her to marry him someday. And up until last week, she had been certain she was going to say yes.

So what if he did not have a stellar chest? Other qualities were so much more important. Refinement. Intelligence. Reliability. Gentleness.

"I'm sorry," she said. "I guess I keep thinking of Shelby."

His hand stayed on hers, and he leaned forward. "Amanda, I hope you aren't getting attached to that child."

She stared at him. How could one not get attached to a child? "Oh?"

"It's just that you've already lost one child. And this one is a heartbreak waiting to happen."

She stared at his kind features, aghast. How could anybody look at Shelby and call her a heartbreak waiting to happen?

"Perhaps I prefer to see her as a bud waiting to bloom," Amanda said.

"Amanda, I appreciate your romantic nature, but I'm a realist, my profession requires that of me. Her family's going to turn up. Someone from her family. And it's going to be the kind of family that puts a little girl on a bus with a packaging label. And you're going to have to give her up to them."

She knew he was right, and she hated his pragmatism in the face of that child's need. Still, she felt a ripple of fear and panic. She wasn't handing Shelby over to just anybody. Fletch had to know that when he dropped her off, didn't he?

As if reading her mind, Woodall said quietly, "I'm surprised at your ex-husband. How could he do this to you? It seems to me it takes insensitivity to a brand-new level. But then if he was perfect, I guess you'd still be married to him, right?"

She could not believe the anger she felt at Woodall's casual assumptions about Fletch, even if they might be somewhat accurate. Maybe it had been insensitive of him to leave Shelby with her. Maybe he hadn't thought beyond the moment, any more than she had. Maybe, just like her, he had put that child's needs ahead of his own feelings.

She remembered that part of Fletch with a sudden hard ache. It had been part of his strength, to look after the needs of others without considering his own.

Amanda had been on the ground with half the town the day he'd gone up the water tower after Harry Jones, who had just broken up with Lydia Stevenson and had decided to end it all. From below him on the ladder, sixty feet above the ground, Fletch had taken hold of Harry's ankles.

"Okay, Harry," he'd said, with unbelievable calm. "You go ahead and jump. But you're taking me with you. I want you to remember I've got a brand-new baby at home."

How terrified she had been. She'd wanted *him* to remember he had a brand-new baby at home, to not take those kinds of risks.

Later, Fletch had shrugged it off. "Harry's a good man," he'd said. "Just temporarily heartbroken. He might have been capable of killing himself. But he sure as hell wasn't capable of killing me."

Fletch's courage had always been a double-edged sword, the thing Amanda loved about him and hated about him in equal turns.

Now, she found she was not without courage herself. She spoke carefully, "Woodall, I would hope that the death of my daughter has not made me the kind of person who is afraid to get attached to a little girl who needs me. Maybe Shelby won't be here next week. Maybe she won't even be here tomorrow.

"But she needs me right now. She needs me to love her without fear, without holding anything back right now. That's why Fletch left her with me."

"Because he knows how well you love," Woodall said, a little sadly. "No ulterior motive at all?"

"Such as?" she said a little coolly.

"I heard a rumor last week."

No kidding. That little kiss by the side of the highway had probably been the hottest topic of conversation in Windy Hollow for days now. Thelma Theobald could be counted on to see to that.

"Really?" she said blandly.

He looked uncomfortable. "Something to the effect of you and Fletch being romantically involved again. I get the feeling the whole town has been waiting for the spark that will begin the wildfire. I think they're laying odds at the pool hall."

As if he knew anything about what was going on at the pool hall. "And do you want me to comment on this—er—pool hall gossip?"

"No, of course not. I guess I just need to know," he paused, and then said carefully, "do you care about him, Amanda?"

There it was. And there was the answer. No doubt. No hesitation. No room for negotiation.

"Yes."

"Oh."

"You cannot share the experiences we shared and not care deeply for that other person, Woodall."

Woodall looked crushed.

"Will I ever go back to him?" Suddenly the no she wanted to say was caught somewhere in her throat. Her sudden uncertainty seemed so unfair to Woodall. And to herself. Damn Fletch Harris.

"I don't think so," she said firmly. It was not an out-and-out no, but it was the best she could do.

The ride back to Windy Hollow seemed strained, quiet, despite the music.

They hit one more yard sale they had scheduled, even though Woodall usually didn't like going in the afternoon. A seasoned garage saler, he liked to be the first one there when the sale opened.

He stopped the car, and turned off the engine.

She went right to the stuffed bear sitting in his own wicker chair. He was huge. Almost as big as her. Light brown, and rotund, and huggable. He looked brand-new.

She bought him, and then looked around. Here a doll carriage in good repair, and there a beautiful doll with a wardrobe to go with it. Real toys. She felt blissful as she paid for her purchases.

Woodall was worried about the doll carriage scratching his trunk.

"Where to?" he asked.

"Can we pick up Shelby, and then go home?"

He didn't look pleased. "You know, Amanda, your life does seem to be becoming somewhat intertwined with theirs. Your ex-husband. His grandmother. What am I supposed to make of that?"

Once, she would have rushed to reassure him, but she felt rebelliously disinclined to apologize for the fact that Shelby had necessitated a few changes in her life.

For once in her life she was going to please herself. She couldn't wait to show Shelby the bear and the doll.

They pulled up in front of Teresa's house, and she hopped out of the car. "I'll just get her."

To her dismay, instead of conducting the orchestra, he got out of the car, too, and followed her down the walk to the back of the house where they could hear voices.

Teresa and Shelby and Fletch sat at a small table at the back. The table was neatly covered, and at the center was a huge platter of cookies, and a frosted pitcher of lemonade. The table and the chairs were obviously much too small for Fletch, a child's set, but despite how cramped he looked, he seemed to be enjoying himself immensely.

Amanda noticed they were eating and drinking from plastic doll dishes, and she smiled when Fletch's huge hand closed around his thimble-size teacup, and he swallowed his lemonade in one sip.

The conversation stopped as the group at the table noticed her and Woodall standing at the corner of the house. She moved across the lawn toward them, Woodall at her heels.

Fletch unfolded himself from the chair and crossed his arms over his chest. He was every inch the cop as he scowled menacingly, as if Woodall were a criminal, and not a man of some stature in the community.

Fletch had a smudge of dirt across his cheek that made him look as rugged and fierce as a warrior.

Woodall strode forward, missing the signs that it was not a good idea, and thrust out his hand. "Dr. Woodall Lamb," he said. "Woody to my friends."

Woody? Amanda stared at him. No one ever called him Woody. Certainly she had never been invited to. Suddenly she felt so angry with him. First, he'd tried to make himself bigger than Fletch by using his title, and then condescendingly let him know he could just be one of the guys if he had to be. Woody, indeed.

"Dr. Lamb," Fletch said, taking the hand. His voice and eyes were ice.

She saw from the sudden pained expression on Woodall's face that Fletch squeezed just a little too hard. Woodall withdrew his hand, looked at it sulkily for a moment, then thrust it into his pocket.

Amanda introduced him to Teresa, but he didn't offer his hand again, just bit out an insincere, "Charmed, I'm sure," and then brightly, "Shall we go?"

"Oh, no," Teresa said. "Shelby is only half-done planting her little garden. You two go ahead, Fletch can run Shelby home later."

Shelby was nodding vigorously.

"Actually," Amanda heard herself saying, "I think I'll stay, too. I'll just see, er, Woody to his car."

Woodall turned abruptly and marched back up the walk, wordlessly removed the bear, the baby carriage and the doll from his trunk and set them on the sidewalk.

He stood looking at her, his expression pained. "I won't call," he said finally. "You seem to have a few things to sort out. But you can call me, if you need me, if you decide…" he let it trail away. "I know I'm not a demonstrative man, Amanda, and I have my faults. I feel a fool for that little 'I can fit in with the working class' charade I did back there, and that you so clearly saw through.

"I've never been jealous before," he said, and

grinned weakly. "I don't think I've ever cared for someone quite the way I care for you."

He grabbed her suddenly by the shoulders, and pressed his mouth hard against hers.

She wanted to feel something. She desperately needed to feel something. Maybe not fireworks, but a little *pop*.

But of course, she had a different kiss to compare it to.

She could not avoid the truth of it. Woodall's kiss, on a scale of one to ten, rated a minus eleven.

Amanda stood on the curb and waved goodbye, and then put the doll in the carriage, balanced the huge bear on top, and went down the walk into the backyard.

She began to hum "The Teddy Bears' Picnic."

Shelby spotted her coming with the toys, and she let out a squeal, before she cut it off abruptly. She raced over and took the bear, staggered under the size of it, giggled and fell on top of it.

"Amanda's new boyfriend," Fletch said, walking toward her. "At least he's got hair."

"Pardon?"

Fletch stopped a few feet from her, folded his arms over his immense chest, and glared at her through narrowed eyes. "You heard me. Somehow I thought you could do better than a two-hair comb over, Mandy."

"Bald men have more testosterone. It's a proven fact."

He looked at her narrowly. "Really?"

"Yes."

"More testosterone than what?"

"Than you!"

"I don't believe you, Mandy Pandy. Did you know the tip of your nose always gets red when you lie?"

"It does not."

"Shelby, hide Amanda quick, before Santa comes to find her. Look at her nose, he might mistake her for Rudolph."

Shelby peeked out from under her bear, looked at Amanda's nose, and squealed with laughter.

He moved toward her, his intent in the darkening of his eyes.

"Fletch, you promised."

"What did I promise?"

"That you wouldn't. Touch me again. Ruin my life."

"Maybe what I'm going to do is keep you from ruining your life. That man is pretentious and dull and about as exciting as day-old porridge."

"That's a lot to know about a man in a single meeting."

"I'm a cop. I specialize in snap judgments."

"And lie detection. Has it ever occurred to you that you might be wrong?" she challenged.

He shook his head, took another step toward her. She moved one back.

"Besides," he said softly, "you challenged me. What's a red-blooded man supposed to do when his testosterone levels are questioned?"

"Fletch, this caveman routine will not work. It will not make me love you again."

He stopped as though she had hit him.

His eyes suddenly swam with pain, and he turned and walked swiftly away from her.

The truth slammed into her just as hard.

No, he did not have to make her love him again.

Because she had never stopped.

Chapter Seven

Childish, Fletch chided himself. Who was he to make judgments about Amanda's new man? His comment was exactly why they weren't still together.

Speak now, pay later. One of his greatest flaws: that inability to keep his mouth shut when it might be better to do so.

Okay, the guy was a wimp. Fletch had known that even before the dead-fish handshake, had known it from watching the good doctor pick his way across the lawn. Pigeon-chested, no muscle tone. And that hair. Couldn't Amanda see Lamb was too old for her?

And what about the fact Doc didn't like kids? That had been evident in the way he had glanced at Shelby, looked right through her as if he hadn't seen her, as if she didn't exist. Was Amanda aware of that? She'd always had a tendency to be a bit naive about people, to overlook the signals they were sending out loud and clear.

My friends call me Woody.

Yeah, right. Fletch had had a juvenile impulse to give him a nice solid punch to that gone-soft midsection, and say "I'm not your friend and never will be."

Of course, being the law, he had to behave himself. If only he could manage to apply his behavioral standards to his mouth, instead of blurting out exactly what he thought of the guy, and exactly what he thought of her and the guy together.

The truth was, it wouldn't have mattered if the guy was The Terminator. Fletch still would have only seen the gap in the teeth, only heard the accent, would have only seen all the reasons he was dead wrong for Amanda.

Four years. He should have been a lot closer to letting her go.

So why was a little temptation forming in the back of his mind? Sic the guys on Doc Baldy. A ticket there. A citation here. They could probably drive him out of town.

But that was being childish again.

And that wouldn't make her love him again, anymore than being a caveman would.

How could she ever love him again?

He'd blamed her for Tess's death.

The fact that there was no one who had escaped his blame did not make that any more forgivable. He blamed everyone under the sun starting with himself, up to and including the paramedics, the day care, the world and God. No one had been exempt.

A stone in a playground. A child swallowing it and choking.

How could he have blamed people for that? Because if someone could be blamed, then the world could be controlled.

Out of the corner of his eye, he saw Amanda and Shelby stuffing the bear into one of those teeny chairs, killing themselves laughing when he insisted on toppling over, the chair stuck to his bottom, again and again.

"Fletch," his grandmother said, suddenly behind him, though he had no idea how she had gotten there, and he didn't consider himself the type of person who it was easy to sneak up on, "go over there and finish your lemonade."

"I've had enough lemonade, thanks." As if it was possible to ever have had enough of his grandmother's fresh-squeezed lemonade.

She wasn't buying. He pretended not to notice the hands go to the hips. He was in for it now. He applied himself to the shovel. "You're over here sulking."

He wasn't going to dignify that with an answer.

"And you're digging that hole clear through to China. It's only a bleeding heart, for Pete's sake, not a thirty-foot blue spruce."

He glowered at the hole he'd been digging, but paused for only a moment. If he turned and faced her, she would know things he didn't want her to know.

"You're mad that she has a man," his grandmother guessed.

She knew anyway. More furious digging seemed in order. The one person who had never been on the receiving end of his temper was his grandmother. It made her dare to go where angels would fear to tread.

She laid her hand on his arm.

"If you feel that way," his grandmother said, her voice full of kindness, "don't let her go without a fight. I've never met a Harris who would go down without a fight."

"If I feel what way?" he said. The hole was really getting ridiculously large. His grandmother could put in a swimming pool if he kept it up.

"Don't you try to pretend with me. I know you still love her."

He flinched, and shoveled, dirt flying, his muscles bunching, the sweat running down his neck and under the collar of his shirt. And even in his discomfort at being pinned down by his mind reader grandmother, he had a renegade thought.

He hoped Amanda was watching. She'd always had a weak spot for muscles.

He took off his shirt and cast it aside.

"That's more like it," his grandmother said with satisfaction and he felt ridiculously transparent. Did she miss anything?

"She already told me she doesn't go for the caveman stuff," he growled between shovelfuls of dirt.

"She did?" his grandmother said, with shrewd interest. "What exactly did she say?"

"I don't remember." He threw the dirt so hard it went over the neighbor's fence. His grandmother made a little tut-tut noise.

"Yes, you do."

"Okay, okay." He mimicked Amanda's voice. "The caveman routine will not work. It will not make me love you again."

"Oh, my."

Another shovelful went over the neighbor's fence, but he was aware he was listening, suddenly acutely interested in what his grandmother's take on Amanda's remark was. That "Oh, my" was loaded with something he had evidently missed.

"Don't you think," his grandmother said sweetly,

"that might mean some other routine, other than the caveman routine, might work?"

He grunted. He didn't do *routines*. He was just about as raw and real as they came, take it or leave it.

He reminded himself Amanda had left it. No, that wasn't exactly accurate. He had done the leaving.

"Fletch Harris, you get over there and drink the rest of your lemonade, before you allow that stubborn streak to completely ruin your life."

He tossed more dirt over the fence.

"Besides, if you keep it up, Edith will be over here complaining about the mess you've made in her yard."

He threw down the shovel, glared at his grandmother and reached for his shirt.

But she was just a little too quick for him. She had that shirt scooped up and rolled into a ball quick as a wink. "I noticed a stain on this," she said. "I'll launder it before you go."

Feeling stupidly self-conscious, and determined not to let it show, he strode back over to the table.

The bear had finally been persuaded to sit upright.

Shelby's face lit up when he came back over to them and she carefully poured him a thimble-size teacup of lemonade. In the face of that, he couldn't very well swill down the half glass he'd left over here and go back to his hole.

It was going to take the whole afternoon to get through the jug at this rate. Which gave him time to think of a routine different than the caveman routine.

Deliberately, he lowered himself into the chair. He picked up the cup and he lifted his pinky away from the tiny glass, took a dainty sip, and in a poor imitation of the Queen's accent, said, "Oh, good-o. Could I have a spot more?" He looked at the bear with astonishment. "Have I met this gentleman before? He's a rather grizzly fellow, isn't he?"

Shelby laughed, real sound. Out of the corner of his eye, he saw Amanda's cautious expression melt into a reluctant smile.

Shelby topped up his cup.

He studied the bear, and whispered to Shelby, "Really, I don't know why you've invited this chap. He has no manners. He's come to have tea with the princess, and—" he lowered his voice even more "—he's not dressed!"

Shelby snickered and pointed at his own naked chest.

He sipped, looked down at himself with astonishment, and said, "Good grief, I seem to have lost my shirt. I don't think I should be having tea with the princess without a shirt."

He became aware of Amanda trying not to look at him, studying the flowers and her fingernails, and sneaking little peeks all the same.

He deliberately curled his arm, making his biceps leap the next time he lifted the teacup to his lips. No mistaking it, her eyes were glued to him now. He lowered the arm, keeping the tension in the muscle, very slowly.

"Most improper," he said, and gave a deep, and heartfelt sigh that just happened to fill his chest.

Amanda was blushing.

Remembering.

It had always been so easy to get her hot and bothered. It was one of her most charming qualities.

He bet Woody couldn't do this.

Childish.

Well, what the hell. It was enjoyable.

He reached up and shielded his eyes with his hand, letting the muscle in his shoulders ripple, tensing his hand just enough to let his forearms cord.

"Oh, where oh where could my shirt be?"

Shelby was looking around the yard, and back to him. Amanda's eyes were darting around, skittering from her lemonade to Shelby to the goofy teddy bear.

But her eyes always came back to him.

Flicked over him, heated, and then moved hastily away.

He should be ashamed of himself for enjoying this charade so immensely. And maybe he was, but certainly not enough to stop.

He twisted in the tiny chair, this way and then that, knowing it would show off the washboard muscles of his abs, the flatness of his hips. She used to trail her tongue over those muscles.

"Fletch, how do you stay in such great shape?" she would ask. "You eat ice cream for breakfast, for God's sake."

"A superior specimen of a man," he would tease. Now he said, "Do you see it, Shelby? Do you see my shirt? It's a fifty-dollar shirt."

She shook her head.

"It's a sweatshirt with no arms," Amanda pointed out.

Now how on earth did she know that? Must have been watching.

He sighed, and held out his teacup. "More tea, please. I think the wicked witch took it," he confided, leaning toward the little girl and flexing his hand on the teacup so that his biceps leaped once again. Amanda liked biceps. She liked that little vein that ran from the inside of his down to his elbow. With a subtle motion, he turned that to her.

He cast Amanda a look out of the corner of his eye. She licked her lips and looked away, looked back, looked away again.

"I'm afraid if I don't get a shirt soon," he whispered loudly to Shelby, "I might be mistaken for a caveman."

He cast Amanda a look from under his lashes. Her lips were twitching, whether from suppressed laughter or from annoyance, he couldn't quite tell.

"I'm not a caveman, you know," he told Shelby sadly. "I'm a very refined gentlemen."

Amanda snorted.

He looked at Amanda, head-on, for the first time and realized he was going about this all the wrong way. He had won her with strength before.

But the strength had proved to be false, no deeper than those muscles he had flexed.

Her strength had been deeper and more abiding. Her strength had been in her ability to feel, and to accept her feelings.

Could he try that? Could he try just telling her what he was feeling for once in his damned life instead of trying to hide it from her?

"I was a knight once," he said slowly.

Amanda didn't look away.

"And maybe I still am. Only now I'm a knight without armor." The next words flowed past all those barriers, right from his heart. They came out of him as though they had been waiting for years. Four years. "So now I'm vulnerable, and not at all sure how to ward off the spears and arrows the world throws at me."

How had this happened? How had it gone from fun, to this, in the blink of an eye?

Amanda's eyes filled with a fine film of moisture.

He ordered himself to turn it back to fun, but he couldn't. That voice from his heart wouldn't shut up now that he'd let it out once.

"Not at all certain," he said, slowly, "how to win the fairest lady of the land. Again."

The moisture became a tear, that slid down her cheek. He reached out and caught it with his fingertip, touched it to his lip.

Shelby, aware of a larger drama, was looking between the two of them, confused and bewildered.

"Fletch," Amanda choked out, "you can't. It's too late."

But suddenly he knew it wasn't. She had stayed here in his grandma's backyard, hadn't she? Even when the doctor had expected her to leave with him? Fletch caught her fingertips with his hand, turned her hand over and kissed the top of it.

He glanced up through the fringe of his lashes and saw her mouth had fallen open in shock. She snapped it shut.

His kiss lingered. He felt her trying desperately to tug her hand away, but he held firm, turned it over, kissed the inside of her wrist. Her skin was soft, sensuous as silk. He felt the faintest tremor where he had his hand locked around her lower arm. She couldn't resist him, he thought with satisfaction.

The liquid hit him in the face, a curtain of cold.

He released her hand, straightened and shook himself. Amanda had thrown her lemonade on him. Couldn't resist him, indeed!

When Fletch met her gaze, expecting to see fury in

her eyes, that wasn't what he saw. He saw terror. Not terror of him, physically. But terror of her own reactions, her own passion.

She was terrified of the very same things as him. Being hurt again.

She wanted him to be mad that she had doused his amor with lemonade. She wanted him to leave her alone. She wanted not to be so vulnerable to him as she was, and she wanted him not to know she was vulnerable.

How could they have done this to each other when they loved each other so much?

But he was not going to back down. The lemonade and ice had given him one message, but her heated eyes on his naked chest had given him quite another.

He leaned forward and picked a handful of ice cubes off the tablecloth, winked at Shelby who was looking back and forth between them, uncertain if this was a game or a fight.

Oh, it was a game.

The greatest game of all.

The dance between a man and a woman who were meant for each other.

He got up. Amanda read his intention in his eyes, and got up so quickly she knocked her chair over.

He noticed she had kicked off her sandals under the table and her feet were bare.

She took off across the grass, as fleet, as nimble, as graceful as a deer. Did Amanda understand, as clearly as he did, that she was not running from him, so much as from herself? From the part of herself that wanted to give in? He wanted the storm that raged between them to give way to the sweet, cleansing rain. He heard

Shelby laugh, mistakenly thinking he and Amanda were playing.

If Amanda wanted to be the deer that was fine. But he was the wolf. Determined. Aggressive. Cunning. He caught her in the corner of the back fence. Trapped her. She watched him come, her chest heaving, knowing she had nowhere left to go.

With one hand on her shoulder, he pinned her to the fence, and then slowly, deliberately, he dropped what was left of the ice down the prissy V in the front of her blouse. While she squirmed, he held her there, not letting her shake the ice out.

Then he felt something cold go down his sock.

Finally, Amanda laughed, giving in to the pull of the past when they had been young and playfulness and laughter had filled their days.

He looked down. There was Shelby, stuffing ice cubes in his socks, shrieking with fiendish glee.

He howled with pretended outrage, and took off after the little girl. Amanda broke from the fence and ran, and he saw her head for the hose.

Just as he lifted the little girl above his head, shouting dire threats over her laughter, the ice-cold spray from the hose hit him.

He put Shelby down, turned and glared theatrically at Amanda. Then he walked right into the spray, letting it cascade down his naked chest, no hesitation as he stalked toward her.

He reached her and wrestled the hose away from her.

She darted away and used Shelby as a shield. He lightened the spray and tried to direct it over Shelby's head.

My, he liked what was happening to Amanda's shirt. It was getting very see-through.

He could see the lace pattern of her bra right through it. Shelby broke away and he let the stream fall on Amanda. She tried to run, slipped in the wet grass, and slid right through the mounds of dirt that surrounded that freshly dug hole he had just done.

He walked over, just as she flipped herself right side up. She was covered in mud from the roots of her hair to the tips of the hem of what had once been white trousers.

"Let me help you clean up," he said, chivalrously directing the hose on her.

The ungrateful wench grabbed his ankle, and suddenly, he was attacked from behind at the very same time.

He toppled into the hole on top of Amanda, bringing the hose with him. Under different circumstances he couldn't help thinking this had the potential to be a very erotic experience, the mud slithering over both of them, he already half-naked, and for all the protection her shirt was offering, she might as well have been.

Amanda apparently wasn't seeing things in quite the same light. She picked up a handful of mud, and shoved it in his face. Shelby leaped into the hole with them.

Amanda planted herself right on his chest and slapped the mud into his face before he could catch her wrists.

Shelby took advantage of his hands being full to ply him with great fistful of mud.

Suddenly the three of them were all collapsed in a heap together, laughing uncontrollably, as if they would never stop.

His grandmother came out of the house and surveyed them, hands on her hips.

He looked at Amanda. Only the whites of her eyes showed through the mud. Shelby's new outfit didn't look new anymore.

His grandmother said, "Now, that's more like it."

It was more like it. It was as if his life had become a little piece of heaven and he suddenly wanted it to last forever.

But of course, he was a big boy now. He should know good things didn't last forever. He would have settled for another ten minutes, but that wasn't to be, either.

"Fletch," his grandmother said, apologetically, "you're wanted on the phone. The station."

He pulled himself away from the circle of their warmth, reluctantly. It was his day off, so if he was being called it was urgent.

Regretfully, he went into the house, cringing at the footprints he was leaving on his grandmother's floor.

There had been an accident on Pillar and Fourteenth. A bad one. One person dead, another clinging to life. Drunk driving involved.

Just like that he was pulled from one world to another.

He poked his head out the back door. "I've got to go," he said. "But save some of that mud for me." He raced home, oblivious to the mess he was getting on his seats, showered and changed in record time.

He was at the scene within minutes. Upon his arrival, he would normally have taken over, and he saw there was an expectation he would do that now. But he saw that the men there were doing everything that had to be done, with calm and composure in the face of chaos that made him proud of them. He realized he was not much of a leader if he did not know when to let go and let others exercise their abilities.

He saw his job as a leader was to do so much more than take charge. It was to prepare others to lead, to take on responsibility, to become independent. If he did his job right, they would not just become as good as him, they would surpass him.

Fletcher wondered if there was hope for him as a team player after all.

Instead of taking over the scene, he volunteered for the difficult job, the one they all hated. On his way to make *the* call, the one that never got easier, he glanced at his watch. He knew he wasn't going to make it back in time to play in the mud, or even to tuck Shelby in, her new bear beside her bed.

Outside the house, a little square box just like his grandmother's, he rested his head against his wrists, his hands on the steering wheel. It didn't matter how long you were a cop. The call never got easier.

Finally, he got out of the car, and went up the walk. He knocked at the door, straightened his tie and took a deep breath.

The door squeaked open a crack. She was old and nervous of opening the door to a stranger.

"Mrs. Bartholomew," he said, "it's me, Fletch Harris." He could tell the uniform was reassuring her and scaring her at the same time. "You play cards with my grandmother," he said to make himself more human in her eyes.

She opened the door all the way, and he saw the fear in her face, saw her bracing herself. A cop didn't appear at your door with your name bearing good news.

"I'm afraid I have bad news," he said, gently.

Once, a long time ago, when he was young, and he

hated this job more than any other, he would have blurted it out and run.

Now he saw her swaying on her feet, her fist pressed to her mouth, her eyes wide with shock and terror.

He opened the door that separated them.

"Gertrude, isn't it?"

She nodded numbly.

He took her shoulder and gently turned her, guided her to the worn couch she had probably shared with her husband for the past fifty years. That man was now dead.

She sat down, and he sat down with her. He told her. They sat in silence for a long time, and then he heard that dreadful moan of pain and loss come from a place in her so deep there were no words.

He covered the worn old hand with his. She began to sob.

It was an hour before he could leave. She had questions, some of them that she asked over and over, forgetting she had already asked them. He made her tea and called her sister for her, and waited for the sister to arrive.

He was just going down the walk when Mrs. Bartholomew came out onto her front porch and called him in her shaky voice. "Officer?"

"Fletcher," he corrected her gently.

"Thank you."

He had just told her her husband was dead. It seemed to him it took extraordinary grace for her to be able to thank him.

"Thank you for staying. And for holding my hand."

"You let me know if there's anything else I can do for you."

"You're a good boy, Fletcher Harris. This town is lucky to have you."

He contemplated that as he went into his darkened office and turned on the light. When had that happened, exactly?

When had he turned from a wild boy, full of himself, to a calmer kind of man, a man who could actually feel compassion for another person's pain? Who didn't walk away from the toughest job of all? Caring for other people.

And suddenly he knew.

Tess.

This was his gift from Tess.

He opened his drawer and looked through it for a long time. There it was. Right near the bottom. Face-down.

A picture of her in a frame, his beautiful Tess. It was a head-and-shoulders shot, one of those portrait things that Amanda had done every time the photographer came through town. Fletch didn't like them generally. The hairdo so perfect, the clothes so fancy, the child so posed.

But this photo had been special. The photographer had blown bubbles and caught the wonder and joy in Tess's huge green eyes, as she had watched one drift upward.

He put his lips to the picture, and then touched his fingertips to her cheek. And then he set the picture on his desk, where he could look at it every day.

Even if it brought up feelings.

It was then that he noticed an official-looking envelope from the state lab on his desk.

He opened it reluctantly.

As he'd suspected, it was the DNA results he had asked for on a sample of his hair and Shelby's.

She was not his.

He felt enormous relief and enormous sadness combined.

Relieved that he had not betrayed Amanda in that final way. He did not think he had, had hoped beyond hope that at least he knew that about himself. But there had still been those few nights in that black hole that had been his despair that he could not account for. Mornings he had woken up in his car, or on someone's floor, his head pounding, not sure where he was, or what he had done.

But at the same time that he felt relieved, he also felt a terrible sadness. Part of him had wanted desperately for that little girl to be his. An excuse to love again, to give himself over to that most terrible and exhilarating of risks, caring about another person.

Part of him had known if he was that child's father he would have had something he and Amanda could share together, something to draw them back together.

He remembered his grandmother's words. If he wanted her, not to give her up without a fight.

But he wrestled with this remaining doubt—did he deserve her?

His office phone rang. It was his grandmother. He glanced at the clock on the wall across from his desk. It was after eleven.

"What are you doing up?" he asked her affectionately. "Not enough hours in the day for you to get all your meddling done?"

She chortled. "Something like that. Actually, I was over with Gertrude Bartholomew. We've played cards together for over forty years. She's beside herself. I helped her make some of the phone calls. Put the casseroles in the freezer."

He closed his eyes. How he remembered that, the constant stream of people arriving on his and Amanda's doorstep, always with a parcel. A casserole.

"Do they think we want to eat?" he'd finally bellowed at Amanda, after one of their well-meaning neighbors had left.

She'd shaken her head. "Someday we will want to eat. But we won't want to cook. They're showing us they love us," she'd said quietly, "that they will be there for us any way they can be. They're baking their love for us right into these offerings."

How differently he and Amanda had seen the world.

"Are you still there?" his grandmother said.

"Yeah."

"I thought I better tell you before I forgot. Shelby talked to me today."

"What? Why didn't you tell me sooner?"

"Because she said it was a secret. I couldn't very well march out to you with her right there and spill her secrets. I'm not even sure I should now. She trusted me."

"You know you have to tell me what she said," he told his grandmother sternly.

"Oh, don't go pulling your cop routine on me. I'm telling you because I think you can be trusted with it, not because you're ordering me around."

He bit back his reply and listened.

"Shelby said her mother is really sick. That she's going to go to heaven. That she picked you to be her daddy."

"Who picked me? The mother or Shelby?"

"The mother."

"How did she know me?"

"Shelby didn't say."

He swore, and his grandmother tsk-tsked.

"Did she say anything else? Where she was from? Her last name? Who her father is? Anything?"

"No, that's all she said. She said her mommy told her she had to be very careful what she said, and she was so scared she would say the wrong thing that she decided not to say anything at all."

He marveled at the child's inner strength. To be able to make a decision like that, and stick to it. "Did you ask questions?"

"No."

"Why not?"

"Trust is a fragile thing, Fletch. You don't push it, or rush it."

It seemed to him she might be talking about more than Shelby at the moment.

"Okay," he said, hearing her.

He hung up the phone, and looked through his stack of papers on his desk. There it was. The composite drawing of Shelby's mother, made by a police artist and the woman in Stevenson who had sold her the bus ticket.

He could see hints of Shelby in it—in the shape of the eyes, in the magnificent bone structure.

But he could see sickness in it now, too. The terrible thinness, the dark hollows under the eyes.

He looked at the clock, and went to the outer office. He didn't usually use the fax machine so it took him a couple of minutes to figure it out.

He faxed the picture to every hospital in Montana. And then Idaho. And then Wyoming. Finally, swaying from exhaustion, he left a note for Jenny to finish in the morning.

He went home and went to bed.

And he wondered, just before he slept, what it would have meant, in terms of his relationship with Amanda, if he would have learned much sooner in his life that it felt better to share power than to have it all. That it felt so much better to be a part of a team rather than the loner who led it.

Then for the first time in a long time, he slept without trying, memories of laughter and mud-covered faces lulling him into a blissful never-never land.

Chapter Eight

Amanda couldn't sleep. She could feel a restless energy burning through her, an energy that had started to tingle as soon as Fletch had taken off his shirt under the bright spring sunshine, as soon as she had seen the familiar ripple and jump of his muscles.

But his words haunted her even more.

I was a knight once. And maybe I still am. Only now I'm a knight without armor.

She was glad the child was sleeping in her spare room upstairs, or she might have gone to him. Gone to him in the dead of night, wanting what only Fletch had ever given her.

That feeling of passion rising—every inch of skin surface tingling, heart racing, breast heaving. That feeling of being on fire with life. That feeling, after the loving, of lying safe and warm and cherished in the circle of his arms. That feeling that the world could not get any better than this.

And maybe she wanted him to take from her the

thing he had never allowed her to give him before: her strength, her compassion, her understanding.

Amanda wandered into the kitchen. She poured some milk into a glass and put it in the microwave.

She reminded herself, sternly, this is who she was now. A woman who drank warm milk to help her sleep, not a woman who slept because her passion had been satiated.

A woman who would go upstairs and put on her flannel pajamas, and read a chapter or two out of a book all about the romance she no longer had.

As she sat down with her milk, she reminded herself she had experienced the flame and fire. And been burned by the untamable white heat of it. She reminded herself it was really much better to read about it in books. Safer.

That was what she wanted now. Safety. Security.

Or that was what she had wanted a week ago. Now it seemed about as appealing as that old spittoon.

"It's still what I want," Amanda said firmly, out loud, as though that would make it more true.

So, if it was what she still wanted why hadn't she protested when Woodall had said he wasn't going to call her? Why hadn't she gone with him? Why had she stayed at Teresa Harris's with Fletch in such close proximity?

And why had she played? Played until she was breathless with laughter, and her shirt was clinging to her indecently like a second skin?

She took a another sip of the milk, and smiled, remembering the unfettered joy of running around the yard with Fletch.

Fletch had always had that gift. He could turn the mundane into the memorable in a flash. The most ordinary moments could become drenched in excitement when Fletch was in the vicinity.

Everyday things—making pizza, mopping the floors, mowing the grass—all those things were things she had done side by side with him. She could still hear the air ringing with their laughter as he tossed his pizza crust and it stuck on the roof, as he overturned the bucket and skated across the wet floors in his bare feet singing and sloshing, or as he turned off the mower, that heat in his eyes, and laid her down on the fresh mown grass.

A little moan escaped her.

Embarrassed, determined not to think anymore thoughts like that, she turned on the radio, hoping for a little late-night music.

Tchaikovsky would do. Deaden this feeling inside of her. Chase away that realization that haunted her every waking moment. She had never stopped loving him. It seemed like a terrible possibility that she never was going to. The choice was not whether to love him or not. In that decision she seemed to have no choice.

The choice was whether to give in to her love for him.

The news came on the radio, and just before she went to another channel, she heard them talking about the accident that had called Fletch away from a sun-drenched afternoon playing in the garden.

The reporter said one man was dead, another person was severely injured, and yet another would be charged with drinking and driving.

Poor Fletch. To have to go from the pure magic of that afternoon to the grim reality of twisted metal, shattered glass, broken lives.

She'd seen, so often, how these things affected him. He never said a word, but she could tell when he had handled something dreadful. He would come in, his whole posture rigid from holding in the pain, even his eyes hooded.

He'd never tell her anything beyond one or two words. Accident. Robbery. She got her details from the radio and the newspaper just like everybody else in town.

She realized, suddenly, with startling clarity, the mistake she'd made. She had let him get away with that. Not telling her. She had let him carry his loneliness and pain inside him.

She'd let him believe he was protecting her by not sharing what had happened to him. Now, in the warmth of her kitchen, sipping hot milk, she looked more deeply at the possibility that the fabric of their marriage had really begun to unravel there. Because when that bigger pain had come, he had handled it the way he handled all his other pain.

Alone.

Shutting himself down. Shutting her out. Had he been trying to protect her then, too?

A knock came at the door, softly.

Her heart leaped. Had he brought his pain to her, after all? Did this afternoon's sweet memory linger with him as it did with her?

Her heart in her throat, her feet dancing, she tried to mask her eagerness as she flung open the door. And then tried to mask how crushed she was that it was Woodall who stood there, and not Fletch.

"I saw your light on," he said. "I've been at Emergency. Dreadful accident."

"I know."

"Oh, yes, you would have heard." The coolness in

his tone indicated he assumed she'd heard it from Fletch and not over the radio.

She could have corrected him, but she didn't. For a woman who claimed to want only safety and security, she recognized she was moving closer and closer to the edge.

"I won't be able to sleep right away," Woodall said, "and I remembered several of my CDs were here. Would you mind if I picked them up?"

"No," she stood back and let him come in. "Are you okay?"

"About the conversation you and I had this afternoon?" he asked.

"No. About the accident."

"Oh, that." He waved a hand dismissively. "Of course. I mean it's upsetting, but I've always managed a certain professional detachment. I have to. I would be crazy if I didn't."

She looked at Woodall closely, and realized it was true. Aside from the fact he needed a few hours to unwind with music, he would not carry this inside him into tomorrow or the days after that.

It was ironic, that Woodall with his kind eyes and his mild demeanor, who seemed like he would be the man most likely to not bounce back from dealing with tragedy, was in fact the one who could.

She knew, suddenly, that's what Fletch had never managed. He'd never managed to be professionally detached. Oh, maybe he had managed the cool look of uncaring, but his job and the things he had to deal with had torn him apart. Because he was passionate about life, and he could not turn that passion on and off.

That inability left scars on him.

All the things she could have done to make it better

for Fletch, and she hadn't. She felt a huge oozing of regret within her as she trailed Woodall into the living room.

He didn't look at her, but sorted through CDs, carefully setting aside the ones that were his. He looked longingly at her stereo, which he had helped her pick.

"I know this is awkward, Amanda, but would you mind terribly if—" He stopped. "No, never mind. Totally inappropriate."

"I find it hard to believe you would entertain an inappropriate thought," she said gently.

"Well, I was just wondering if you'd mind if I listened to a few CDs here. The treble on this stereo is magnificent. Much better than mine. I'll use the earphones."

She stared at him and felt a smile twitch at her lips. Her jilted boyfriend had made a midnight call and he was interested in her stereo? What had she let her life become?

She had found, finally, a man whose passion had an off switch. Only he'd forgotten to turn it back on.

There was such a thing as too safe. And it was possible to go back and make right the things you had done wrong.

Who would have ever guessed Woodall would be a messenger from the gods?

"Actually, Woodall, you'd be doing me the favor. I have something I need to attend to tonight, and I can't leave Shelby alone."

"Something to attend to? In the middle of the night? You?"

Oh, Woodall, you missed the secret side of me, the best side of me entirely. It was the part Fletch had never missed, had always drawn to the surface.

And it was Fletch drawing it to the surface now. Her wilder side. Her bolder side. The part of her that wore lace instead of flannel.

Fletch had always been about passion.

"It's an emergency. Someone needs me," she said.

He gave her a long look, then put on his CD. Without another glance at her, he adjusted the headphones, then went and lay down on her couch, one arm over his eyes. "Shelby won't wake up will she?"

"I don't think so."

"Go, then. Gallivant. See if I care."

Gallivant. She smothered a giggle. "I'll only be an hour. Thank you, Woodall."

She was crazy, she knew that. It was absolutely crazy to be doing this. But she'd been sane for long enough.

Had it gotten her her heart's desire? She wanted to be with Fletch. She wanted to take his pain and hold it, share it with him.

No, she did not just want to be with Fletch, she *had* to be with him.

She pulled a light sweater over her T-shirt and jeans, slipped out the door and down her walk. The night was beautiful, scented, the black of the sky pierced with bright pinwheels of light from the stars.

She breathed deeply for a moment, then got in her little bright-red VW and put it in gear. The car was about passion, too. Woodall thought it was awful. That the color screamed, and that the car was pretending to be sporty. He thought a woman of her stature should be looking at a nice Volvo.

The doubts assailed her as she turned off her drive and onto the main road. What was she doing? What if she didn't have a clue what to do or say once she got there? What if he turned her away? What if he thought she was a prowler and shot her?

Not one of those doubts made her do the sensible thing and turn around.

She knew he lived in the cabin on the outskirts of town, down by the river. It had been in his family for a long time.

Together, they had dreamed of fixing it up one day, having it as their summer place. When Tess was older and knew how to swim—an unpleasant irony how protective they both had been of Tess.

She drove through the dark, deserted town, and finally pulled into the winding, rutted drive. As she pulled up in front of the cabin, his vehicle was there, but there was not a sound, or a light or a movement.

She got out of her car, shut the door and stood there breathing deeply. The river had a scent of its own, clean and mysterious. She liked the sound of it.

She ordered herself to come to her senses, to get back in her car and go home to Woodall. Last chance.

She noticed the moon was full and blamed her madness on that.

She turned toward his house and went up the stairs. Should she knock? On impulse she tried the door. The handle twisted under her hand and the door creaked open.

A cop who didn't lock his door. She stifled a nervous giggle and stepped into the kitchen. She reminded herself that he had a gun, that it might prove dangerous to go creeping around his place in the dark.

"Fletch?" she called softly, as her eyes adjusted to the dark.

The cabin was as she remembered it, except that now it filled her with sadness. It was tinier than she remembered, and she was not sure how he had managed to make such a small space seem so empty. A card table, one chair.

One chair. Didn't he ever have company? One of the guys over for a beer after work? It had been four years since their divorce. Hadn't he ever brought a woman home with him?

She found herself selfishly hoping he hadn't. That, just like her, no one had ever shared his bed since. That he was ruined in the same way she was.

The rest of the inventory was quick because there was nothing: no throw rug on the worn tile, no pictures, not even a calendar on the old graying log walls.

The sink overflowed with dishes, but other than that, it looked tidy. Barren and bleak, but tidy. Wait. A small engine had been pulled to pieces on the kitchen counter.

"Fletch?" she called again, softly.

In the stillness, she heard his deep breathing. She crept into the bedroom that adjoined the kitchen and stopped. Moonlight poured in a wide-open window, and the scent of the river mixed with the scent of him, strong, wild, manly.

Fletch.

The moonlight flowed over him like translucent silver water. He had a single sheet tangled around his lower body, the blanket on the floor.

He was sleeping on his stomach, his head resting in the crook of his right elbow. His left arm was by his side. His hair had that rooster tail sticking up at the back of his head, and she longed to go and smooth it down.

But she didn't move. She drank him in. He looked like a masterpiece in sculpture, his broad beautiful back painted in moonlight, the ridges of his shoulder blades etched in silver and black, his face in deep shadows.

She felt she could just stand here, forever, and drink in the beauty of him, the strong cast of his features, half-shadowed, the thickness of his lashes, the slight part of his full lips.

After a very long time, she dragged her eyes away from him and looked around the tiny room.

Like his kitchen, it had a certain unlived-in look about it. A chair in the corner had his uniform draped carefully over it. There was a bureau without a mirror and without a single adornment. No photographs, no knickknacks, no curtains, no rugs. Dead center of the room was a heap of unwashed laundry, topped by the mud-stained jeans from this afternoon.

How could she have let this happen to him?

How could she claim to have loved someone and let them put themselves in this prison of bleak loneliness?

She reminded herself she had tried. She had tried so bloody hard to hammer down the wall that kept getting higher and higher around him.

She had tried to be there for him.

And he had turned away. He had found solace in substances and in isolation, instead of in her.

The pain of that came back to her, fresh.

But looking at him, lying there so still, in this bleak room, she suddenly knew that any pain he had caused her was minuscule in comparison to what he suffered himself.

She saw his gun hanging from the holster belt on the bedpost, and she went, very carefully, and moved it out of reach.

Then she untangled the sheet and pulled it up gently

around him. She gathered the blanket off the floor and
tucked that around him, too, even though he seemed
oblivious to the coolness of the breeze coming off the
Bitterroots tonight.

He slept on.

She gazed at him for a moment, uncertain exactly
why she had come, uncertain what she should do next.

The longing to be with him was greater than her
confusion.

She kicked off her shoes, took a deep breath and
lifted the sheet. She slid under it. She could feel the
heat from his body, the rise and fall of his chest. Something sighed within her, and she nestled into him. His
arm closed around her, gently, possessively, protectively as if they had never been apart.

His skin felt wonderful, warm and silky and springy.

He smelled so good.

Her eyes closed. She would stay only a few minutes.
She would not even awaken him. In a moment her
sanity would return to her, and she would go home.

She would go home with one more piece of Fletch
to hold within her.

He would never know she had been here, that the
moonlight had made her mad briefly, insanely.

Deliciously.

She closed her eyes.

''Mandy?''

Her eyes flew open. Sunlight was streaming around
them. Fletch was up on one arm, looking at her with
drowsy confusion.

Fletch in the morning. Whisker-roughened face.
Copper-colored skin against white sheets. Muscles relaxed and beautiful.

She leaned toward him, and then pulled back. And then way back!

She leaped from the bed.

"Good God," she said, looking for her shoes, running her fingers through her tangled hair, looking anywhere but at him.

"Mandy, what are you doing here?" His voice was deep and sleep-raspy. Sexy. It sent tingles up and down her spine.

Why didn't he sound judgmental? Shocked? Why did he seem only mildly curious, as if he had expected this to happen?

She combed her fingers frantically through her hair, then shoved her feet into her shoes. "I came to tell you I'm getting married," she blurted out, a drowning woman reaching desperately for the lifeline that would save her. From him.

From the seducing power of being with him. In the same room.

His gaze became narrow, and though his voice was calm, she could hear the hardness in it. "What would your fiancé think of the way you spent the night? In the bed of your ex-husband?"

"That was an accident! I came to tell you, and you were asleep, and—" Her voice floundered. She had to get out of here. She was a terrible liar and she was just making everything worse. She turned, but not quickly enough.

Her wrist was caught in an iron grasp, and he pulled.

She sat down on the bed with an ungraceful thump. She tried to stand back up, but he was beside her, had her face between both his hands.

She was free. She could get up and run now.

But she didn't.

She stared at the light in his eyes, and sighed. And surrendered. "Kiss me, Fletch," she whispered. "Please."

And he did, his tongue finding her tongue, his hands moving from her cheeks to her shoulders, drawing her closer to him.

She was not sure if the roaring she heard was the river or the blood rushing to her brain. Flooding her brain.

She couldn't even think anymore.

Of anything except this.

And how right this was. His lips on hers. Claiming her. Possessing her.

"Why did you really come?" he whispered huskily, his lips on that sweet spot on her neck that only he knew about.

"I'm going to get married," she mumbled stubbornly.

"No, you aren't. Or at least not to Doc Baldy."

Did that mean Fletch might ask her? To marry him again? Oh, God. She couldn't. But how could she live without this?

How had she managed to live without this?

Right now it felt as if she had been sleeping, a sleeping princess, waiting for his touch, his kiss to bring her back to life. Her prince. Her knight.

"Why did you come here?" he asked again, pulling slightly away from her, looking at her.

"I couldn't sleep last night. I—I came here because I—I wanted to ask something about Shelby."

"Really?"

She covered her nose. He smiled, a slow, sleepy sensuous smile and she knew he didn't believe a word of it.

He kissed that soft spot on her neck, ran his tongue down it.

"I heard some of the details of the accident on the radio," she gasped. "I was worried about you."

"You were worried about me, Mandy Pandy? Why? I wasn't in the accident. Just cleaning up the mess after."

See? He would always be the same. Locking her out.

"Oh, never mind, I have to go."

But she knew she wasn't going anywhere until he said so. Until his lips stopped moving, until his hands stopped caressing.

"I had to tell Gertrude Bartholomew," he said quietly.

She stared at him, and hope flickered.

"She's my grandmother's age. Frail as a bird. And I had to tell her the man who had come home to her for fifty years wasn't coming home anymore."

"Oh, Fletch."

He didn't shrug it off. He didn't turn away from her. He looked her full in the face and said, "It was rough."

The phone rang.

"Ignore that," he said gruffly.

"Shelby!" she cried. "I left Woodall with Shelby. Oh, my God, he'll be beside himself. He's probably called the police. That's probably your office now, reporting me missing. And you'll say I'm here, and the whole town will know!"

Fletch, his eyes never leaving her, rolled over and picked up the phone. "Yeah? It's okay, Grandma, she's here. Okay, I'll remember."

He hung up the phone, propped the pillows behind him, looked at her. "Your doctor friend dropped Shelby at my grandmother's, who called to report you missing. She won't tell anyone else." He paused, his look more intent. "Does he spend the night at your place often?"

"No! Not that it's any of your concern. Oh, I've worried people needlessly. What was I thinking?" Her eyes drifted to his lips. "I've got to go. Fletcher, I have to go. Right now." *Before I do something crazy. Crazier.*

He patted the bed beside him.

She had to go, but she didn't. She went and sat, primly, legs out in front of her, back against pillows, right beside him. Ridiculously she felt as if she needed to fill the space between them with words. "So," she said conversationally, extraordinarily aware of his naked chest inches from her, "What did your grandmother say? When you said, okay, I'll remember?"

He smiled. "She told me it was bad manners to answer my phone 'yeah' and was it so much harder to say hello?"

Amanda laughed nervously. Was he flexing his muscles on purpose? He was. He was doing that thing with his biceps on purpose. "What did she think about me being here?"

"If she thought anything about it, she didn't say. What you should be worried about is what I think of you being here."

"Oh." He slanted toward her, and his shoulder touched hers.

Fire leaped through her veins and swept through her skin.

His lips touched her neck. "I think," he growled, "you're here for this." And then he took her mouth.

It was not just his passion in that kiss. It was his

pain. She felt something in him, some vestige of control relax.

Sweetly. Sweetness becoming light. Light becoming brilliance. Brilliance becoming her sun and her moon and her life and her love.

She kissed him back.

And everything that had been lonely within her melted into everything that had been love. Everything that had been broken within her became healed. Everything that had been incomplete within her became whole.

The phone rang.

"Don't get that," she said.

"I have to," he said, reluctantly. "It's my private line with the station. It's something important."

What could be more important than what they were doing?

She supposed all kinds of things. Death and destruction. Bad guys with guns. Good guys getting shot at. She sighed and let him go.

He reached for the phone again.

And when he put it down she could tell by the look on his face they weren't picking up where they had left off.

He had that cold, shuttered look about him.

"I have to go," he said, and then he hesitated. "They've found Shelby's mom."

She felt as if the color were draining from her world. Hadn't Woodall tried to tell her? This was a story with no happy ending?

Why hadn't she listened?

Why hadn't she listened to every single thing Woodall said? If she had, she wouldn't be sitting here right now, begging for kisses. She'd be at an antique auction, or listening to music and planting flowers in her garden.

Shelby gone.

How was that possible? She had just come. And Amanda realized, suddenly and sadly, how completely she had given herself to that little girl.

How much she had allowed herself to believe again that good things could happen and that they could happen to her.

Watching that little girl with her enormous enthusiasm, hadn't she really begun to do the most dangerous thing of all?

Not just believe.

No, sir. She had to take it that step further. She had started to believe in miracles. That she and Fletch could make it after all. That love could repair the damage between them. That somehow that little girl would be the link to the things that were meant to be for them.

He was already up out of the bed, tugging on the uniform pants that were so neatly laid over the back of the chair.

He pulled a fresh shirt from the closet, and she watched it, envied it, as it slid over his skin. And then the heavy gun and holster.

Going away from her.

He glanced once back at her.

And what she saw in his eyes before he looked swiftly away changed her for all time.

She saw he was afraid.

She contemplated that for a moment. Fletch, afraid. Fletch who seemed to be courage and strength personified, afraid.

Of what?

Of losing another little girl.

And of losing her, Amanda, all over again.

His fears were the very same fears as her own. How could something that they shared be driving them apart?

It had happened once. Was she going to allow it to happen again?

"I'm going with you," she said.

He turned, glanced briefly at her, then scanned the floor. He got down on his hands and knees and fished under the bed until he came out with a pair of socks.

He sat on the bed, his back to her, pulling on the socks. "No."

"I'm coming with you."

"I said no."

"You know, Fletch, we did it all by your rules last time, and look where that got us."

His gaze flicked to her, and she saw they had another fear in common. They were both afraid to hope.

"I can't take you with me on official police business."

"Is that right? You didn't even hesitate to drop that official police business off on my doorstep, did you?"

He didn't say anything to that.

"If we're losing her, Fletch, we're losing her together. And we're going to hold each other up through it. Do you hear me?" She heard the strength in her voice, the resolve.

And waited to see if he could accept her on those terms. Bolder than she had been before, braver, better.

He stared at her, then ducked his head, fished under the bed again and came out with a highly polished black boot. Intently, he pulled the laces tight.

And in such a low voice she had to strain to catch the words he said, "Yes, ma'am, I hear you."

Chapter Nine

Fletch pretended to be concentrating on lacing his boot, but the truth was, if he tied up that lace any tighter they were going to have to cut off his leg. He sneaked another look at the woman who sat on the other edge of the bed. Her hair, no matter how often she combed her fingers through it, looked incredible.

Wild and tangled and like the hair of a woman who had experienced a little more than just a kiss. Her blouse and her trousers were rumpled, that veneer of sophistication she wore around her like armor was getting thin.

He'd said he heard her. But now she had to hear him.

He straightened, finished with the lace once and for all. He had to know if this was about him or about Shelby. It amazed him how far he had come even since last night.

Because last night, when he had opened that DNA

lab test, he had hoped the girl was his. And now he saw that wasn't what he wanted at all.

He didn't want Amanda to care about him solely because they had accepted responsibility for that little girl together. He didn't want Amanda to care about him because she thought he had a chance of being appointed the guardian of Shelby.

"Shelby isn't mine," he said quietly. "I'm not her father."

If that was her motivation, that should kill it dead. Without being that child's father he had as much chance of being appointed a guardian as a snowflake in hell.

"Oh, Fletch," she said, waving her hand at him with something that looked suspiciously like annoyance, "do you think I don't know that?"

He stared at her, folded his arms over his chest and planted his feet. "How can you know that, when I wasn't certain myself until around eleven o'clock last night?" He thought she would say she had been watching Shelby and seen they weren't alike.

He had been doing that, looking for a small mannerism, a crinkle of the nose or a twinkle of the eye that he might recognize Harris in. But it had not happened.

Instead, she said, "You were always more willing to believe the worst of yourself than I was."

The words wrapped around him, softly, like a blanket thrown over a freezing man. He wished, desperately, for a few more minutes or a few more hours to explore this thing that was happening between them, that had brought her to his bed and laid her down in it beside him.

That had brought them to this place, where she had

just uttered those magical words, so casually, as if she was unaware of the healing power of them.

You were always more willing to believe the worst of yourself than I was.

But if it was those words that brought healing, it was the other thing she said that brought hope. *We did it all by your rules last time, and look where that got us.*

"Does that mean," he said slowly, carefully, "that the marriage you came here to tell me about has been, um, postponed?"

The last of her sophistication died under the fiery red of her blush.

He smiled, and she did, too. And then he laughed. And she did, too. And it was so wonderful for them to be in a bedroom laughing together over rumpled sheets that he was almost able to forget that nothing had happened.

Nothing.

And everything.

She had said it didn't work last time. Which meant there was going to be a this time. Didn't it?

Maybe if they were playing by different rules than last time, he just had to ask if he wasn't certain what something meant, instead of guessing. Maybe his guesses had been wrong—way wrong—all the time. Maybe her throwing herself into work after Tess hadn't been about her rejecting him and moving on without him.

Maybe it had been about healing herself. What kind of man would deny her that, take it personally?

The kind of man who couldn't even clarify what something meant.

"So," he said, bending and fiddling with his other lace, "does that mean there is going to be a this time?"

She ducked her head, too. Played with her shoe, too. But when she looked up, he saw the fiery determination in her eyes.

"Yes," she said, firmly, and then her eyes grew very round, as the enormity of what she had said registered. Suddenly businesslike, Amanda said, "Before we leave, I need to see Shelby. It may have worried her that I wasn't there this morning."

"Especially since the doctor was," he said, unable to strip the sourness from his tone.

"Why would he worry her? He's such a nice man."

If her future lay with Fletch, could she think other men were nice? It occurred to him that really wasn't his decision. A new day for he and Amanda would have to be based in trust. And maturity.

And he planned to start being mature, as soon as he set her straight about the doctor. "He hates children."

"Woodall? He does not."

"He does, Mandy. That man does not want ice cream on the leather of his carseats, or Silly Putty on his stereo."

A reluctant light went on in her eyes. He went over to her side of the bed, pulled her to her feet, kissed the tip of her nose. "But I'm sure he has other sterling qualities. Really."

He decided telling her she could be friends with the doctor would be counterproductive. Because he knew he didn't have any right at all to tell her who she could be friends with. Not now. Not ever. Not even if the future held what he hoped it did. Especially not then.

"How did you find Shelby's mother?" she asked, as they went out the door.

"She talked."

"Shelby?" she said astonished. "To you?"

He smiled at her tone. "No, not to me. I know I'm not what any five-year-old in her right mind would pick for a confidant. She talked to my grandmother. She told her her mother was really sick. Last night I ran some late-night faxes. This morning there was an answer. A young woman named Joanne Higgins is in a hospital in Moscow, Idaho."

"That's a fairly long drive," she said, and he could hear the satisfaction in her voice. She was glad they were going to have this time together. "We have a lot to talk about, you and I."

He had the uneasy feeling she fully intended to tackle the past. And he knew she was right to do it, even though he dreaded it. Until they cleared away the mess in their past, there was no hope for their future.

They needed to talk about where they had been, and where they were going. They needed to figure out what they both wanted, and if it was even close to the same thing.

Maybe Amanda leading was not such a bad thing. He would have been tempted to talk about other things. The weather. Mutual friends. The new baseball diamond.

Fletch Harris had not said a prayer for a long time. But he found himself praying now. That he and Amanda were going to the same place and wanted the same thing. And he didn't mean that was in Moscow, Idaho.

They arrived at his grandmother's, and Shelby was delighted to see them.

"I'm sorry I wasn't there when you woke up,"

Amanda said, taking the little girl in her arms and covering her with kisses.

Loving her even though they had moved that one step closer to losing her. He contemplated that for a moment.

And knew a difficult truth.

Through their entire relationship he had accepted the role as the strong one, the one who would handle everything, the one who would be in charge. Had he missed her strength entirely?

Even without tragedy, could their relationship have survived if he did not recognize this truth about Amanda: that she was as strong as he was. In some respects, she was stronger. He could not lead any team she was on.

It would have to be a partnership of equals.

His grandmother was watching Amanda and Shelby, a smile on her face. "I don't think she has to worry about that little mite. I don't know where Shelby has been or what she's been through, but whatever it was has given her gifts. She's as adaptable, as sturdy and as tough as a dandelion."

Was this another truth about life? That the hardest times a person survived gave them gifts?

What if Tess's gift to him and her mother was that they would come to know each other completely? Not the romantic illusions, but the real strengths and weaknesses underneath all that? Couldn't a relationship go deeper and stronger than a man had ever dreamed if he could find a place where he could truly be himself?

A place where he could be, not just strong, but weak, too?

A place where he could admit he did not know or have all the answers?

Shelby had run over to him, and he lifted her high until she laughed with delight. As he pulled her down from the air, she put her arms around his neck, pulled herself into him, hugged hard and tight. She whispered something to him and his eyes filmed over.

The little girl had called him Daddy. And he was not sure if that was what the future held. A reminder that he and Amanda were about to confront the future.

Together.

And suddenly he was so glad of that.

He quickly ran Amanda home so that she could change. He waited in her kitchen, taking in all the little details that were so Amanda, allowing himself to look, and to feel what he had not allowed himself to feel before here.

He felt at home in this space.

For a man who had not been certain he would ever feel at home anywhere again, it was like having a long, cool drink after crossing the desert.

He got up from her table and went over to the little rocking horse. A horse that needed a child to make it magic. A horse that just looked like a cow unless there was love there.

He knew he was getting way ahead of himself. Picturing other babies, he and Amanda's children filling this kitchen, his life. He took a deep, steadying breath and closed his eyes.

And then Amanda was beside him, touching his arm.

"Fletch, are you all right?"

He looked down at her, at the warmth and concern in her eyes, and he saw her love for him.

And prayed again. For God to let him be the man he needed to be. This time, the man she deserved.

"I'm all right," he said gruffly, and then he remembered he wasn't going to do that anymore, and so he said more honestly, "I don't know if I'm all right or not."

It was a four-hour drive to Moscow, and if he thought she'd been pushy on the way to Belleview, it didn't even compare to this.

"You didn't like it when I went back to college, did you?"

He thought maybe she should have started off with something a little more neutral than that, but he reminded himself he wasn't quarterbacking this round.

"I never said that," he hedged, looking at the determined set of her chin and drumming his fingers on the steering wheel.

"That was part of the problem. You never said *things*. You hinted. You were sarcastic about my getting an education. But you'd never just tell me what was on your mind.

"Okay. I hated it."

"But why?"

He didn't say anything for a long time. And then he said, "I wanted to be enough for you. I wanted to be your whole world, just like you were mine."

"I wasn't your whole world! You had the world's most challenging job."

"Well, I still wanted to be your whole world."

"So, it was okay for you to have found what you were meant to do with your life, but not for me?"

"I hoped what you were meant to do with your life was love me. And Tess."

"That is hopelessly old-fashioned. Not to mention self-serving."

"Well, I am! Hopelessly old-fashioned. Completely

self-serving." He took a deep breath. "I was scared, Mandy. I was scared that I wasn't giving you everything you needed. That you wanted something more than a rough-spoken logger turned cop could ever hope to give you. I thought you wanted to walk in a world where I could never go. Where people ate with the right fork, and talked about books I wouldn't understand and listened to music I didn't get."

"Oh, Fletch. Why didn't you just tell me that? I could have told you in a second it wasn't so."

"I don't know why I didn't tell you. Maybe I didn't know that's what it was myself. A feeling that I was completely unworthy of you. You're the one who said it, Mandy. We were so young. We were out there, flying high, doing a high-wire act with no net. It was exhilarating, it was incredible, but neither one of us had a clue what we were doing. We just flew without a set of instructions and trusted our love would be enough."

"I remember believing that," she said softly. "That our love would be enough to erase all the differences between us. Enough to compensate for the fact we only communicated in bed."

"That isn't true." He thought about it, and said less certainly, "Is it, Mandy?"

"I think it is."

"Is that such a bad place to communicate?"

He liked it when he made her laugh, and she laughed now. "No, I don't think so. But if we were going to grow together, we had to have more."

"Such as?"

"You had to be willing to share your life with me, Fletch. And you weren't. Even before Tess you were shutting down and shutting me out. And after—"

"I did everything wrong, I know. I blamed you. I said if you'd stayed home, maybe it wouldn't have happened."

Her face had gone white with remembered pain.

"Mandy, did I ever tell you I was sorry I said that?"

She shook her head, mutely. She turned away from him, her face to the window. He knew she was crying.

He quietly pulled off the road, then gathered her in his arms and stroked her hair. "I hope it's not too late to tell you now. I'm sorry I said that. I never meant it.

"It just seemed if I could make the whole thing preventable, then it could have been controllable. So, I wished you'd stayed home or I'd stayed home. I wished so many things, and I couldn't turn back the clock and have even one of those wishes come true.

"All my life, anything I wanted, Mandy, even you, I just turned the force of my will on it, and I got it.

"And then all of a sudden I found out how inconsequential a man's will can be. I found out I really wasn't in control of the world at all. I was powerless to keep Tess safe. And if I was powerless to keep her safe, how could I keep you safe? Especially since you weren't partial to listening to me, to all the ways I could have made your world smaller, so that I could be in control of it.

"All my life, I'd always had this kind of faith. I mean it wasn't churchgoing faith, but it was a faith in the order of things. That spring followed winter, night followed day, and parents died before their children.

"After Tess, I couldn't trust the world anymore. And I couldn't trust myself to love that deeply, ever again. I came to terms with the fact that my love was not enough to protect the people in my world.

"That was my job, Mandy." He choked on his own

emotion. "That was my job," he said again, his voice hoarse. "To protect people. And when I couldn't protect the people I loved the most, it nearly destroyed me.

"I didn't want to love you anymore. It felt like my helplessness was killing me. So instead of admitting I couldn't hold back fate if it had a terrible plan for you, I left you.

"But I never stopped loving you, Mandy. I wanted to. I begged myself to. But I couldn't. Even though I knew you were better off without me, and that I had failed you in every way, I couldn't stop loving you.

"I left you hoping I could at least stop you from loving me."

She had her arms around him. Pulling her to him.

He felt the strength in her. A kind of strength he had never had. And he gave in to it. He did the one thing he had never done in all his life.

Fletcher Harris surrendered.

After a long time, his tears washing down her shirt, her grip never lessening in intensity, she whispered, "Do you remember? The wading pool you bought her? But you didn't want to buy the pump. It took you three days to blow it up."

He didn't want to do this.

He didn't want to go there. He didn't want her to see him weak, but when he tried to pull away, she held on tighter.

She said, "Remember when we put her in it, for the first time? Remember the look on her face?"

And he remembered, and the tears came harder and faster. But Amanda just kept talking. About the time they'd gotten lost in the Bitterroot mountains, and it had made them late for Tess's baptism, and how they'd

stood in front of both their families and half the town
in their hiking clothes with twigs in their hair, giggling.

"Do you remember?" she said over and over.

The first birthday cake, and the ill-fated puppy, and
their hopes and dreams and foibles and victories. She
made him remember, until the tears turned to laughter.

And then she said, "You got stuck somewhere,
Fletch. You got stuck on the day she died, and you
forgot all the wonder she brought us, all the happiness.
Don't you see? You honor the time she spent here by
not forgetting what she was in every single moment
before that one where she put a rock in her mouth.
Fletch, you have to remember. You have to.

"For me."

"And for me," he said.

"And for you," she agreed.

"You didn't tell me. If you forgave me for blaming
you."

"Fletch, I knew you were blaming everyone and everything. And I knew the truth you never saw."

"What was that?"

"That you loved like no one else I had ever been
around. Ever. You're greatest strength was your
greatest flaw. You loved with everything you had.

"How could I have ever condemned you for loving
so deeply?"

He leaned his head on the steering wheel and took
deep gulps of air. He wiped the tears from his face
with his sleeve. Finally, he started the vehicle again,
pulled back onto the highway.

Amanda was silent now. She only moved closer to
him, so that her shoulder touched his, and he could feel
her fingers in his hair.

They stopped for lunch, and he remembered this

about her more than any other thing—the ease of being with her. How he never had to think of clever things to say or be, how with Amanda he just was.

They came, finally, to their destination, but somehow he felt they had arrived at exactly where they needed to be before they got to Moscow.

He got out of the car, took a deep breath and tried to bring himself into a professional mode of mind.

He was here on official business.

The woman in there had abandoned her child.

But it was so much more complicated than that. How could it be called abandoning when the child had come to the people who needed her most in the world?

"Fletch," Amanda said softly, "don't try and figure it all out right now. Let's just go see her. Talk to her."

He nodded, and even though it might not look good or professional when her hand found his, he let it stay there.

Her real name was Joanne Higgins, and the nurse who showed them filled them in on her prognosis. Shelby's mother had untreatable cancer. The doctors felt she had less than two weeks to live. The nurse led them to her room, then looked at him sternly.

"You're not to tire her out, do you understand?"

He nodded, and Amanda smiled at the nurse. "Don't worry," she said, "I'll look after him."

I'll look after him.

They walked into the room. It was dark, the curtains drawn. He generally associated hospital rooms with flowers, but there were none here, and he felt the loneliness of what that said. A sliver of light from the window fell over a frail young woman, her face skeletal it had become so thin. Still, he could see Shelby in her face.

She saw them, and he didn't know what he had expected.

Fear, maybe, or wariness.

But not the joy that lit her face from within when her tired eyes came to rest on him.

It was Amanda who went forward and held out her hand. "I'm Amanda Harris. I've been looking after Shelby," she said gently.

The blue eyes fastened to her face, worried, and then Joanne relaxed. "Is this your wife, Officer Harris?"

"Yes." No hesitation. It seemed like the wrong time for explanations that they were divorced.

"So it did work out," the girl said. "I thought it would."

Amanda pulled up a chair beside the bed and took the young stranger's hand. Such a natural gesture for her.

"Is Shelby okay?" Joanne asked.

Amanda nodded and the girl relaxed, tiny and frail among her pillows.

He pulled up a chair, aware that Joanne watched him with a smile in her eyes he did not understand. He knew this was not going to be like any investigation or interrogation he had ever conducted before. And he was surprised to realize that was okay with him.

"You don't remember me, do you?" she whispered, finally.

"I'm sorry, no."

She smiled weakly. "It was a long time ago, Officer Harris."

"You can call me Fletcher."

"Fletcher. You told me that before. That night. I thought then it was a good name. A strong name. We met, once, you and I, six years ago, in Windy Hollow."

He scraped his memory but came up blank.

"No, you wouldn't remember. It was a chance encounter. A horrible night. Rainy and bitterly cold. I'd had a fight with my boyfriend in Kalispell and left him. I was hitching a ride to Seattle. I'd worked there once. I was hoping…" Her voice drifted off, and then she sighed and said, "Anyway, my ride dropped me off outside of Windy Hollow.

"I was so hungry and so cold and so scared. You see, I was pregnant and had nowhere to go. No money. No man. No family. No nothing.

"Then you came along in a police cruiser, and I thought I was in trouble. That maybe hitchhiking wasn't allowed, or you'd see I was a vagrant and throw me in jail. I was going to hide in the ditch, but you'd already seen me and pulled over.

"You were so big, but as soon as I looked in your eyes, I stopped being scared. I thought, this man is sadder than I am.

"You asked me where I was going, and then told me to hop in the car. You drove me right to the bus station, even though I told you I didn't have any money. You bought me a bus ticket to Seattle. I remember you pulling your wallet out and paying for it with your own money. This picture fell out. Of the cutest little baby. It fell on the floor and I picked it up and handed it to you.

"You told me the bus wasn't coming for an hour, and you took me across the street and bought me a bowl of soup. Do you remember, now?"

"No, I'm sorry. Six years ago was not a good time for me."

"Because your little girl had died."

His head flew up.

She nodded. "You told me. Because I asked about the baby in the picture. I could tell you didn't want to talk about it, and I knew then why your eyes were so sad.

"The bus came, and you put me on it. And all the way to Seattle I thought how unfair life was. Here I was having a kid I didn't want, and you had just lost one that you did.

"Here," she said softly, "you had just lost your baby, and you still had it in you to show me kindness and respect.

"I vowed I was going to be good to my baby. And, you know, I tried my hardest, but things just never seemed to work out. The jobs never lasted, I was always on the move, I had a gift for meeting the wrong kind of men.

"You know, even though I hadn't wanted her at first, pretty soon I couldn't imagine my life without Shell. She loved me and I loved her, and she was the best thing that ever happened to me. She deserved a daddy like you, but that's the one thing I could never seem to give her, no matter how hard I tried.

"So, when the doctor told me there wasn't any hope for me, I knew there was one thing I wanted for Shelby. A daddy like you. And then I thought, well, why not you? We didn't have no one else in the whole world. My folks are long gone. Not one single person, 'cepting Shelby, ever cared about me the way you did that one night.

"And I figured that made you the closest thing to kin that I had.

"I knew if I tracked you down, and just came out and asked you, you'd say no. Why should you take some stranger's kid? But I knew if I sent her to you,

you'd love her. I knew your big old heart wouldn't be able to say no to her, and I was right, wasn't I?''

He felt as if something was breaking apart in him. At the worst time in his life, this fragile human being had seen only good in him.

Before Tess had died he would have never bought a hitchhiker a bowl of soup. It was Tess who had made him into a man with compassion.

Another of the gifts she had given him. Tess, losing Tess had given him maturity, strength and compassion that he had not had before.

It had made him the man who deserved the love of a woman like Amanda.

"So, will you take care of my girl, Fletcher Harris? Please?''

And it was looking into this young woman's eyes that allowed him to see himself as he really was. Not perfect, not by a long shot. But a good man, and a decent one, and one who always gave what he did his very best shot.

Still, how could he take care of her girl? He was a single man. Or maybe he wasn't. Things were unresolved between him and Amanda.

But when he looked at Amanda, he saw the light shining in her eyes beneath the tears. He'd done it by himself long enough. They had to be a team. They had to make this decision together.

He looked at her again, deeper, and something happened that had not happened for a long, long time. He knew what she was thinking without her saying words.

''We'll take care of Shelby,'' he said, and his hand found Amanda's. ''We'll take care of Shelby for as long as she needs us.''

Amanda said, softly, "You know we'll love her with our whole hearts and souls."

We.

"I know," the girl said, and then whispered, "Do you think I could see Shelby one more time?"

He met Amanda's gaze again, and said, "I think we can do a little better than that."

Chapter Ten

"Are you ever going to ask me to marry you?" Amanda had asked. Six months had passed since Joanne, Shelby's mother, had died.

He was lying on her couch, his head in her lap, still in his uniform. Amanda played with his hair, and marveled at the richness in her heart as they shared the simple events of their separate days.

Once Amanda and Fletch had been the best of lovers. Now, amazingly they were the best of friends. She watched every day as the light grew inside him, glowed from his eyes. Every day, the three of them—Fletch, Shelby and her—spent time together becoming the family Joanne had dreamed for her daughter. They finished planting flowers for spring, retired to Miller's Pond on the hottest summer days, raked leaves in the fall. They fixed up the cabin by the river, and took Shelby and Teresa on picnics there.

Every day she thought, Today Fletch Harris will ask

me to marry him. She could feel something in him that she had never, ever felt before.

Contentment.

He radiated contentment. But he didn't ask her to marry him.

When he didn't answer, now that she'd finally asked him about it, she said again, "Fletch? Are you ever going to ask me to marry you?"

"Nope."

For the better part of a second she felt as if the bottom was falling out of her world. And then she noticed the smile in his voice, the light dancing in his eyes.

A light she had thought she might never see again. A boyish light, full of mischief and charm.

"Well, why not?" she asked, giving his shoulder a smart smack.

"Ouch." He rubbed his shoulder. "I asked last time."

She stared at him. "Are you saying you are waiting for me to ask you?"

"Whenever you're ready," he said with a nod.

"I was ready five and a half months ago!"

"Tut-tut. You've never had difficulty speaking your mind before. I'm learning to surrender control, remember?"

"I want to kill you!" she sputtered.

"You want to kill me? On the marriage proposal grading system I'd have to give you a C minus for that one."

"All this time we could have been married," she told him. "We could have been—" she felt the heat rising up her throat.

"In bed together?" he said softly.

"Well, yes, if you want to put it that way."

"You told me we had to learn a different way to communicate," he reminded her, amused. "I'd say we've done that, haven't we?"

She thought back over the last months, and found it hard to regret one minute of that time. Fletch had been the perfect beau. Bringing her out to sumptuous dinners, bringing her flowers, planning so many wonderful outings.

But if Fletch had been a perfect beau, it did not even hold a candle to what a perfect daddy he was. According to Joanne's wishes, he had been made Shelby's legal guardian. He had shouldered this responsibility as if it was his greatest joy. He had told Amanda he planned to adopt Shelby, and she had thought then, for sure, he would propose marriage.

Now, Amanda realized the truth about the delay. They *had* learned to communicate—found a meeting place beyond passion.

"We did everything too fast, last time, Amanda," he said, suddenly serious. "I regretted that. I regretted that I didn't woo you, and wine and dine you and bring you flowers."

"Well, I have to admit it," she said. "I've loved every moment of being wooed by you, but Fletch?"

"Hmm?"

"Enough all ready. Let's get married."

"Better," he said. "Slightly. I'd give you a *B*."

She sighed as he slid his head off her lap and pushed his reluctant frame up to a sitting position. She got down on bended knee at his feet. She took his hand and touched it to her lips. And let her heart speak. "Fletcher Harris, I can't bear it when you walk away from me in the evenings. I live to hear you laugh. I live to see your eyes for the first time in the day. I love the sound of your voice, and the way your muscles move. I love your strength and your calm, and your ability to show me your heart.

"I want to be with you every single day for the rest of my life. I want to marry you. I want us to raise Shelby together, and have babies. Will you marry me?"

"Now that's more like it," he said, with a grin.

"Stay tonight, Fletch."

He shook his head. "I've been carrying this around in my pocket, just in case you ever got around to asking. You'll have to humor me on this one. I'm not staying until this—" he pulled a tattered envelope from his pocket "—is back on your finger."

She opened the envelope, addressed to him in her hand. Her simple wedding band was inside.

"I remember the day I sent this back to you," she said. "I was crying so hard I could barely write your name on the envelope."

"I remember the day I got it. I was going to take it and throw it in the river, but something stopped me. I'm glad now that I didn't. Thank you for saying you will wear it again, Amanda. For giving me a second chance at life. For giving me a gift greater than diamonds or jewels. The gift of saying you want to be my wife. Again."

And then he got up off the couch, tugged her to her feet and kissed her in the way she'd been dying for him to kiss her. A man coming home from his heartaches and pain, laying his weapons at her feet. Surrendering.

"Stay," she begged.

But he said no, that he'd been given a second chance to get it right and he meant to take it.

* * *

It was just a week later, and Amanda watched Fletch moving through her living room, stopping here and there to say a few words to someone, to touch someone else on the shoulder.

Her husband.

They had said their vows in her living room, encircled by the love of family and friends less than an hour ago.

Her husband.

Her light. Her love. Her forever.

She wore a dress of light-blue silk, and she had flowers in her hair.

She had always thought Fletch was so attractive, but today he stole her breath away. He had long since lost the dark jacket, and the tie was unknotted at his throat, the silk shirt rolled up at the sleeves. His rooster tail was sticking up, and the whiskers were starting to darken his cheeks.

He had Shelby on his hip, in the white dress with the pink sash that he had bought her so long ago.

Even then, Amanda had known it was a flower girl's dress. Shelby had her head on his shoulder, her thumb in her mouth, her eyes drooping.

He had never looked so strong.

Fletch, Amanda realized with utter contentment, was her Samson.

Losing Tess had been like cutting his hair.

But when it came back, his strength was more than it had been before. And different. Quieter. Deeper. Not something he had to prove, but something that was him as much as his skin, as much as his smile, as much as the beat of his heart.

His strength was such that he tore the old building

down—the building that held all his beliefs about himself, and all his beliefs about the way things should be between a man and a woman.

His strength was such that he was putting up a new building, better than before, stronger, more able to withstand the inevitable storms that would challenge its integrity.

She saw him greet Woodall and smiled. It was the most unlikely of friendships, but when Fletch had brought Joanne Higgins to Windy Hollow, and settled her in his grandmother's front parlor, Woodall had become her physician.

And the town had become the family that poor girl had never had. It was as if Windy Hollow had been waiting for Fletch to ask it for something, to need them as much as they needed him. But of course, man of steel that he was, he never had.

But when he quietly put out the word that he needed help, people flocked to his grandmother's house. People came to read to Joanne, to hold her hand, to change her bedding. People made her special soups and sometimes, it seemed every flower in Windy Hollow had found its way to that front parlor.

In the end, Woodall was there above and beyond the call of duty. He insisted on being called at any time of the night or day if Joanne needed him.

When it was over, there remained a respect between the two men that went deeper than words and that revealed itself when Fletch asked Woodall to speak at Joanne's memorial service.

There hadn't been a dry eye in the house when Woodall had finished his short eulogy, with the words, "I've heard it said there are angels among us. Joanne was one of them." But he hadn't been looking at the picture of Joanne when he said it.

He had been looking at Shelby, snuggled between Amanda and Fletch, the miracle that had brought them back together.

Windy Hollow's miracle, really. This child had come to belong to the whole town as much as she belonged to Amanda and Fletch. She was the sweetheart of the police station, the mascot of the firefighters, a ray of light and laughter, a ball of energy and curiosity. The entire community was helping the child with her sorrow, helping her return to wholeness, giving her a family so much larger than any she could have had before.

Dabbing at her eyes, Thelma Theobald had introduced herself to Woodall after he had spoken so eloquently at the memorial service.

Down at the pool hall they were taking odds it would never last, but Amanda wasn't so sure. Thelma had done for Woodall what Amanda could never do. Coaxed his passion to the surface. He'd traded in the old-man car, and having defied the odds, they arrived at Fletch and Amanda's wedding this afternoon in a fire-engine-red Dodge Viper.

Now it was midnight.

The last of the guests were gone. Shelby had gone home with Teresa for the night. Fletch was picking up dishes.

"Never mind that," Amanda said. "It's time for bed."

He came to her, scooped her up in his arms and carried her up to the bedroom. He lay her down on the bed, and looked at her with reverence.

He kissed her long and passionately.

It was a kiss that promised things. Ecstasy, but other

things as well. It was a kiss that promised he would be there to watch the stars come out at night with her. And wake up to the morning dawn with her as well.

And he would be there to watch the first snowfall, to build a snowman with Shelby. He would be there with her to watch the little girl blossom into a woman.

He would be there through the laughter and through the tears, through the good times and the bad.

His hands found the buttons of her dress, and she reached for him.

Hours later, they lay in the circle of each other's arms. Exhausted and exhilarated, they watched as the first pink of the new day washed through the window and crept across the bed.

"Look at how the darkness melts before the light, Mandy Pandy," he whispered, awed by the miracle of the new day, a day full of hope and promise.

She looked at his face, where the darkness had melted before the light. And the light had a name.

Love.

Epilogue

The Windy Hollow graveyard sat in a wooded rise
above the river. A black wrought iron fence separated
it from a quiet park with a picnic table. Only the park
wasn't very quiet right now, not since the noisy Harris
clan had arrived.

But Fletch carried a quiet inside himself as he
opened the gate that separated the Harris family plot
from the rest of the graveyard. In no hurry, he stopped
and read the inscriptions on the headstones of his an-
cestors. And his grandfather. And his mother and father.

Finally, he came to them.

Two headstones, side by side. One for a child.

And one for a mother.

They had not been related, Tess Harris and Joanne
Higgins. Joanne was the only non-Harris who had ever
been buried here.

The mother and the child had never met each other.

And yet, even though they had not met, Fletch had

a sense of this mother and this child being linked in ways too large for the human mind to grasp fully.

In the final analysis, he thought maybe it was heaven that decided who was family and who was not.

He heard laughter and looked across the fence. His grandmother was unpacking the picnic basket. Shelby was running with a kite, and now that it was airborne, she was trying to get her little sister, Annie, to hold the string in a chubby fist.

Shelby would be eight soon.

Annie would be two.

He looked at Amanda, her face radiant as she watched the children play and chatted with his grandmother. He could see the round swell of her tummy. In the summer there would be another baby. Amanda hoped for a boy, but he had no preferences.

The miracle of another life was good enough for him.

He heard Amanda shout, and the chuckle of his grandmother. Amanda grew more beautiful every day, glowing with the deep inner beauty of a woman who was cherished above all things.

He would go be with them soon. But first he needed to be here. He opened his satchel and took out his gardening tools. Carefully, he cleared away the weeds and snipped the grass that grew long near the headstones.

Carefully, he dug the soil, as he did every year at this time, and planted the two red geraniums.

Red had been Tess's favorite color.

And Joanne's, too.

As he patted the dirt into place around the plants, he thought, possibly, spring was his favorite time of year.

When he was done, he put down the trowel and sat for a long time, in peace. Unafraid. Stronger in surrender than he had ever been in control.

In the distance, he could hear the song of the river. He remembered thinking during those four years of agonizing aloneness that it was answering a question he did not know how to ask. But he knew what the question was now.

A question all men had to ask themselves at some point in their lives. Was life random, or was there a flow to all things?

The river had been answering him. The rivers ran, the seasons came and went, all according to a larger plan.

He, too, was a part of that plan, and buried in every tragedy that came, he was content to believe there was a reason, a gift, even.

Tragedy had allowed Fletch Harris to travel a great distance in a relatively short amount of time, if he measured time by the ancient flow of the river.

He'd learned that he was not superhuman, after all. He could not leap high buildings in a single bound.

But high buildings only gave men the illusion they were getting closer to heaven. Maybe that was why they built them.

The truth was love—love in all its pain, and all its glory—love forged the stairway to heaven.

"Daddy!" Shelby called, "come help me with my kite. Pllleeassse! Annie, don't slobber on it!"

He got up and brushed off the knees of his jeans, then carefully packed the tools back in the satchel.

"I'm coming," he called. He turned one last time, looked at the headstones, and then tilted his chin and looked up at the rich blue heavens above him.

"Thank you," he said softly, before he walked away.

*   *   *   *   *

You've shared love, tears and laughter.

Now share your love of reading—

give your daughter Silhouette Romance® novels.

Where love comes alive™

*Silhouette presents an exciting
new continuity series:*

**When a royal family rolls out the red carpet
for love, power and deception, will their
lives change forever?**

The saga begins in April 2002 with:

The Princess Is Pregnant!

by Laurie Paige (SE #1459)

**May: THE PRINCESS AND THE DUKE by Allison Leigh
(SE #1465)**

**June: ROYAL PROTOCOL by Christine Flynn
(SE #1471)**

Be sure to catch all nine Crown and Glory stories: the first three appear in
Silhouette Special Edition, the next three continue in Silhouette Romance
and the saga concludes with three books in Silhouette Desire.

And be sure not to miss more royal stories,
from Silhouette Intimate Moments'

Romancing
the Crown,

running January through December.

Where love comes alive™

*Available at
your favorite
retail outlet.*

Visit Silhouette at www.eHarlequin.com

SSECAG

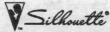

These New York Times *bestselling authors*
have created stories to capture the hearts and minds
of women everywhere.
Here are three classic tales about the power of love—
and the wonder of discovering the place
where you belong....

FINDING HOME

DUNCAN'S BRIDE
by
LINDA HOWARD

CHAIN LIGHTNING
by
ELIZABETH LOWELL

POPCORN AND KISSES
by
KASEY MICHAELS

*Available only from Silhouette
at your favorite retail outlet.*

Silhouette®

Where love comes alive™